J. R. ROBERTS

JOVE BOOKS, NEW YORK

THE BERKLEY PUBLISHING GROUP
Published by the Penguin Group
Penguin Group (USA) LLC
375 Hudson Street, New York, New York 10014

USA • Canada • UK • Ireland • Australia • New Zealand • India • South Africa • China

penguin.com

A Penguin Random House Company

THE SALT CITY SCRAPE

A Jove Book / published by arrangement with the author

For information, address: The Berkley Publishing Group,
a division of Penguin Group (USA),
375 Hudson Street, New York, New York 10014.

ISBN: 978-0-515-15446-7

PUBLISHING HISTORY
Jove mass-market edition / May 2014

PRINTED IN THE UNITED STATES OF AMERICA

10 9 8 7 6 5 4 3 2 1

Cover illustration by Sergio Giovine.

ONE

Clint Adams rode into Hutchinson, Kansas, which had recently acquired the nickname “Salt City.” The discovery of salt, plus the fact that the Chicago, Kansas and Nebraska Railway had built a main line through town, from Herington to Pratt—which would eventually extend to Tucumcari, New Mexico, and El Paso, Texas—had caused great growth in the town since he’d last been there, half a dozen years before.

He was back to check on his friend Ben Blanchard, who, in drilling for oil the previous year, had struck salt.

Hutchinson’s main street was a flurry of activity. The street was filled with ruts and potholes, most of which were filled with water from recent rains. He avoided them so as not to risk Eclipse breaking a leg.

He rode to the livery at the end of the street and dismounted. It had doubled in size since the last time he was there, and as he walked Eclipse inside, he saw three men working. Two were tending to horses, while the other was working over a hot forge.

"I need to put up my horse," he called out.

The three looked at him. They all had the same blank look on their faces, which led him to believe they were related—probably brothers.

"Hello?" Clint said. "My horse?" He was having doubts about leaving Eclipse in the hands of these three.

The one at the forge said, "Danny, take care of his horse, damn it!"

"Sure thing, Zed."

The one called Danny came forward and reached for the reins, but Clint hesitated.

"It's okay," Zed said. "He has a way with horses. They like him."

"Come on, big fella," Danny said, reaching out his hand. Eclipse nuzzled it, surprising Clint. He handed Danny the reins, then removed his rifle and saddlebags before the man walked the big Darley away.

"See what I mean?" Zed said. "I'll bet he bites, right?"

"Usually."

"He'll get along with Zed. That's quite an animal. My brother will see to him real good."

"I hope so."

"How long you stayin'?"

"Don't know," Clint said. "Few days maybe."

"Okay," Zed said. "We'll settle up before you leave."

"Okay with me," Clint said.

"Two hotels right up the street are okay," Zed said. "In case you was wonderin'."

Clint looked at the third brother, who hadn't said a word.

"Does he talk?"

"Nope," Zed said, "not since he was a baby."

"Oh . . . well, okay, yeah, take good care of him. I'll check back in."

"Whenever you like, Mr. Adams."

"You know who I am?"

"I may be dumb, Mr. Adams," Zed said, "but I ain't stupid."

Clint didn't know what to say to that, so he just nodded, turned, and left.

He checked into the Salt Lick Hotel, which looked fairly new. His room was large, with a good bed and a new dresser. He was used to furniture in most hotels that was falling apart. This was a treat.

He looked out the window at the busy street below. He decided to get a meal, maybe a beer, before he went looking for Ben Blanchard's office.

He went back downstairs, onto the street, walked for a few minutes until he came to a small café. He looked down the street, didn't see a likelier place, so he went inside and allowed a waiter to show him to a table away from the window.

Over a steak he thought about the telegram he'd received from Ben. He knew that Blanchard had come to Hutchinson for several reasons. Real estate was one, and drilling for oil was the other. Neither of those things panned out for him, but in drilling for the oil, he'd struck salt. He was now the owner of a large salt mine, and he'd asked Clint to come and take a look at his operation. Clint wasn't a miner—even though he did have a gold mine for a while in Shasta County, California—but he knew Blanchard must have been asking him to come to Hutchinson for another reason.

Not in the habit of refusing to help his friends—especially

when they asked—he was nevertheless not in a hurry to find out exactly what the trouble was. He knew that, once again, he was about to find himself embroiled in somebody else's problems.

Or maybe Ben Blanchard just wanted to show off his operation to his good friend.

Yeah, right.

TWO

Ben Blanchard stared hard at his foreman as the man delivered the bad news.

"We'll have to dig that shaft again, boss," Dennis Mahoney said.

"Any chance it caved in by itself?" Blanchard asked.

"I don't see how," Mahoney said. "We had that shored up pretty good. Naw, had to be sabotage."

"What about our night watchman?"

"I hadda fire him," Mahoney said. "I could smell the whiskey on him."

"Goddamnit, Dennis!" Blanchard said. "I count on you to hire good men."

"And I do, boss," Mahoney said, "when I can find 'em."

At forty-two, Mahoney was ten years younger than his boss, but both were big, beefy men who enforced their rules as often as not with their fists.

"All right," Blanchard said. "I can't blame you if there are no good men around. And we know we can't count on the law."

"What about that friend of yours you sent for?" Mahoney asked.

Blanchard stared at the foreman, who was from the East. Did he really not know who Clint Adams was?

"He's not just a friend," Blanchard said. "Clint Adams is the Gunsmith. Doesn't that mean anything to you?"

"I guess I'll have to pay more attention to these minor Western legends now that I'm living out here," Dennis Mahoney admitted.

"There's nothing minor about Adams," Blanchard said. "He's as big a legend as Wild Bill Hickok. You've heard of him, haven't you?"

"Well, of course. But is he coming? This Adams, I mean?"

"He's supposed to be," Blanchard said. "But who knows when he'll get here. Hopefully, while we've still got a mining operation."

"Look," Mahoney said, "we know who's behind this. Why don't we go and bust some heads? That's what we'd do back in Philadelphia. Isn't this the lawless West?"

"Lawless for some," Blanchard said. "Yeah, we know Avery Kendall is behind it, but he's got the law in his pocket. If we bust his head—or the heads of any of his men—we'll end up in jail."

"Then what do we do?" Mahoney asked. "Just wait for your friend to get here?"

"And try to stay open until he does," Blanchard said. "Find us another night watchman, Dennis. Or stay on watch yourself. In fact, I'll split the watch with you."

"Let me see if I can find somebody before we do that," Mahoney said. "No point in you killing yourself working day and night—or me either."

"Okay," Blanchard said. "Meanwhile, get our number one crew on that shaft. I want it back open by tomorrow."

"That's a tall order—but we'll try," Mahoney said hurriedly, before his boss could yell at him.

After Mahoney had left the office, Blanchard opened the top drawer of his desk and stared at the gun there. He was no hand with a gun, never had been. He was a businessman who had stumbled into this whole salt mine business. But he wasn't about to let Avery Kendall give him the bum's rush without a fight.

He closed the drawer. A gun wasn't the answer. At least, not a gun in *his* hand.

He grabbed his hat and left the office.

When the door to his office slammed open, Sheriff John Cade looked up from his desk. His two deputies turned and stared as Ben Blanchard came charging in. A big man with wide shoulders, Blanchard filled the room, and the two young deputies shrank back momentarily.

"Goddamnit, Sheriff!" Blanchard yelled.

"Hold on there, Mr. Blanchard," Cade said. "Don't come into my office bellowin' at me." He looked at his deputies. "You fellas get out and go to work."

"Yessir," one of them said, and they both left.

"What's on your mind now, Mr. Blanchard?" Cade asked. He was in his mid-thirties, a tall, rangy man who had been wearing the star for about a year, since he beat the incumbent in the election the year before. Rufus Brennan had been sheriff of Hutchinson for twelve years before he lost the election, which he and half the population knew had been fixed by Avery Kendall.

"What do you think is on my mind?" Blanchard asked. "Same as always. Sabotage!"

"Now, Mr. Blanchard," the sheriff said, "you've got to stop throwing that word around. Next thing you know, you'll be tellin' me it was Mr. Kendall who did it."

"Him or somebody he hired," Blanchard said. "Look, Sheriff, I'm coming to you because you're the law . . . even though I know you're in Kendall's pocket."

"Now, Mr. Blanchard," Cade said, "if I was a different sort of man, that kind of talk might get me riled up."

"You mean if you were an honest man?"

Cade smiled and sat back in his chair.

"Suppose you tell me what happened."

"My number one shaft caved in again."

"That happens in mining, don't it?" Cade asked.

"Only this didn't happen by accident."

"Now, Mr. Blanchard—"

"All you've got to do is come and take a look," Blanchard said. "I can show it to you."

"I tell you what," Cade said. "I get the time, I'll come out and take a look at your caved-in shaft."

"If you get the time, huh?"

"Well," Cade said, "I'm really busy."

"Yeah, I can see that."

"Mr. Blanchard—"

"Forget it," Blanchard said. "Forget I said anything. I'll take care of it myself."

"Mr. Blanchard," Cade said, "I got to ask you not to break the law."

"Yeah, I know," Blanchard said on his way to the door. "Consider me asked."

THREE

Clint finished his steak and peach pie, washed it down with coffee, and stepped out onto the boardwalk. At that moment he saw a man across the street, moving fast, almost knocking people over as he went. He had stormed out the door, Clint noticed, to the sheriff's office.

It was Ben Blanchard.

Blanchard was a big man, and even people he didn't physically bump into were pushed aside just by his wake. Clint opened his mouth to shout, but he was too late. Blanchard was out of range.

Clint crossed the street and headed for the office. He could find Blanchard later, probably at his mining office.

As he entered, the man seated at the desk looked up, his mouth open to say something. When he saw Clint, he clamped his mouth shut.

"Sorry," the lawman said. "I thought you were somebody else."

"Oh, you mean that big man who charged out of here?"

"Yeah," the man said, "I thought he was coming back. I'm Sheriff Cade. What can I do for you?"

"I just rode into town," Clint said. "Hope I didn't come at a bad time."

"You mean that fella? No, he's just a complainer. One of those people who's always blamin' somebody else for his problems. You know the type."

"I do," Clint said. "I've met them before. Anyway, my name's Clint Adams."

"Adams!" the sheriff said. He came half out of his chair, then sat back down. "You mean . . . the Gunsmith?"

"That's right."

"Well . . . what brings you to Hutchinson?" Sheriff Cade asked.

"I'm just here to see a friend," Clint said. "I thought I'd drop in and let you know I'm in your town. It's usually better than having the local law find out on their own."

"Well, I appreciate you dropping in and letting me know you're here," Cade said. "I hope you're not here looking for any kind of . . . trouble?"

"Believe me, Sheriff," Clint said, "I'm never looking for trouble. It just seems to find me."

"I can understand that," Cade said. "How long do you plan on being here?"

"I'm not really sure about that," Clint said. "Probably a few days."

"Well, enjoy your time," Cade said. "We got a nice town here."

"Looks like a busy town," Clint said.

"Yeah, it is that."

"Maybe I'll see you at the saloon and buy you a drink sometime," Clint said.

"I'll look forward to it." Cade had been nervous when he first heard who Clint was, but he seemed to have settled down some.

Clint headed for the door.

"Hey!"

"Yeah?"

"Who're you here visitin'?" Cade asked. "You didn't tell me who your friend was."

Clint looked at the lawman, said, "That's right, I didn't," and walked out.

Whatever had happened between the sheriff and Ben Blanchard, it obviously hadn't been good. There was no point in giving away his connection to Blanchard—not yet anyway.

FOUR

Clint assumed that Ben Blanchard had an office in town, so he went looking for it. It didn't take long. It was right on the corner of Main and King Streets. In fact, the sign over the door said, KING STREET MINING COMPANY. Clint wondered why Blanchard hadn't named the mine after himself.

He crossed the street and tried the door. It was locked. Wherever Blanchard had been rushing to, it wasn't the office. He peered in through the window on the door, saw some desks, but no one was working.

He wondered where the mine was.

Blanchard poured himself another shot of whiskey from the bottle on the table.

"The goddamned law!" he swore.

"We know he's in Kendall's pocket," his foreman said. "I mean, we already knew that."

"Yeah, yeah, I know."

"You tried to do the right thing," Dennis Mahoney said.

"Yeah, I did," Blanchard said. "I guess now we're gonna have to try to do the wrong thing."

"What does that mean?" Mahoney asked. "You mean like . . . using Pinkertons?"

"We don't need strike breakers, Dennis," Blanchard said.

"Then what? Your friend? When's he going to get here?"

Blanchard looked at the man who was coming through the batwings and asked, "How about now?"

Clint had tried three saloons, found Blanchard in the third, sitting with another man. He figured the way Blanchard had been charging down the street he was mad, and in need of a drink.

Blanchard stood as he approached the table.

"Am I glad to see you," he said, shaking hands.

"I saw you tearing down the street," Clint said. "I think you came out of the sheriff's office."

"Have a seat," Blanchard said. "This is my foreman, Dennis Mahoney. I'll get you a beer. It's still beer, right?"

"Right."

Clint sat as Blanchard went to the bar.

"Glad you got here," Mahoney said. "He's been waiting and waiting."

"I assume there's trouble?" Clint asked.

"You assume right," Mahoney said. "Lots of trouble."

"With the mine?"

Mahoney nodded.

"We were just talking about it," he said. "He went to the sheriff, but the law is in Avery Kendall's pocket."

"Kendall?"

"He owns everything in town but Ben's mine. He's after that."

"That's an old story," Clint said. "Rich man trying to own everything."

Blanchard returned with Clint's beer, set it down in front of him, and sat.

"Dennis filling you in?" he asked.

"Just enough to tell me we're dealing with an old story," Clint said.

"Goddamned money," Blanchard said. "Why do men with money think they have to own every goddamned thing?"

"I don't know," Clint said.

"I wish I had money," Blanchard said, pouring himself another drink. "Then maybe I could own everything."

"I'd like to own everything," Mahoney said, draining his glass. Blanchard refilled his, too.

"Well, I'm here, Ben," Clint said. "What do you want me to do?"

"Shoot Kendall!"

"Can you do that?" Mahoney asked.

"I can," Clint said, "but I won't. What else?"

"I don't know," Blanchard said. "Prove that he's the one behind the sabotage."

"Maybe I can do that," Clint said. "Tell me about it."

Clint listened intently as the two men related to him all the "accidents" happening in the mine.

"And the most recent was last night," Mahoney said. "Our number one shaft collapsed."

"And it couldn't have happened on its own?"

"Not the way we had it shored up," Mahoney said. "I mean, I know my business. I have a degree from a university back East."

"That's why I hired him," Blanchard said.

"What about security?"

"We had a night watchman," Mahoney said, "but he was drunk."

"He might have seen something anyway." Both men gave him a blank look. "Did you ask him?"

"Actually," Mahoney said, "I just fired him."

"All right, then," Clint said. "That's where I'll start. I'll ask him. Have you hired anybody else?"

"I've interviewed some men," Mahoney said. "Haven't decided yet."

"Well," Clint said, "make sure you hire more than one."

They stared at him again.

"If one falls asleep, the other one can wake him up."

"Hiring two night watchmen takes money," Mahoney said.

Clint looked at Blanchard.

"You have money, don't you?"

"Well . . . some."

"You have a successful salt mine, don't you?"

"Well, yeah," Blanchard said, "but I still have to get most of it out of the ground. That takes money. Then I have to ship it."

"And that takes money," Clint said. "What about your buyers? Aren't they paying up front?"

"Some of them are," Blanchard said, "but only some of the money."

"So you're operating on a shoestring?"

"Pretty much," Blanchard said.

Clint knew Blanchard well, which was why he knew his friend was probably mismanaging the mine operation.

"Okay," Clint said, "I'll start with the fired night watchman." He looked at Mahoney. "You hire at least one new man, and we'll go from there."

"Okay," Mahoney said.

"Agreed," Blanchard said. "I'm glad you're here, Clint."

Clint drank half his beer and said, "Get me another, and then tell me about the sheriff."

FIVE

Mahoney told Clint where the former watchman, Ike Davis, lived. He was surprised to find that it was a house. Mahoney had made the man sound like the town drunk, and they usually lived in places like underneath the boardwalk or the back room of a saloon.

Clint knocked on the door, and a cleanly dressed, freshly washed man answered the door. He was in his forties, with shaggy black-and-gray hair.

"Help ya?"

"I'm looking for *Ike Davis*."

"That's me."

"You're the Ike Davis who used to work as a night watchman at the salt mine?"

Suddenly, Davis looked less friendly.

"Why? Who are you?"

"My name is Clint Adams," Clint said. "I'm just—"

"The Gunsmith?" Davis asked. "You're the Gunsmith?"

"That's right."

"And they sent you here from the mine?"

"I'm friends with Ben Blanchard," Clint said. "I'm just trying to help."

"So whatta ya want from me?"

I'd like to come in and talk for a while."

"About what?"

"About what you might have seen last night."

"Nobody asked me that before," Davis said. "They just fired me."

"Well, I'm asking."

Davis seemed to consider the matter and then said, "Well, yeah, okay, come on in."

Clint entered, found himself in a small one-room house. There was a small bed against one wall, a table and two chairs, and an old stove.

"What'd you think you'd find?" Davis asked. "The town drunk?"

"Well, frankly, yes."

"Yeah, well, that ain't me," Davis said. "In fact, I wasn't even drunk last night."

"The foreman said he found you drunk and asleep."

"So I fell asleep," Davis said. "I been workin' three jobs."

"And drunk?"

"I wasn't drunk. I had a couple of drinks to try and keep me awake. It didn't work. Have a seat."

Clint took one of the chairs at the table.

"I ain't got no whiskey to offer you," Davis said. "Just coffee."

"That'll be fine." In fact, Clint had smelled the coffee when Davis opened his door, and it smelled good.

Davis went to the stove, poured two mugs, came back, and put one in front of Clint. Then he sat down across from him.

"This is damn good coffee," Clint said.

"Yeah, thanks," Davis said. "It's probably the one thing I can do right."

"Well," Clint said, "why don't you tell me what you saw last night, and maybe we can see about getting your job back—and maybe with a raise, so you don't have to work so many jobs."

"That'd be real good, Mr. Adams."

"Did you see anything, Ike?"

"I saw two men," Davis said. "Snoopin' around."

"And what happened?"

"I chased 'em off."

"Did you see who they were?"

Davis chewed his lip, then sipped some coffee so he could think.

"You knew them," Clint said. "Told them to get away, and they did?"

"I thought they did," Davis said. "It wasn't like they was scared of me, or anything."

"But they left."

"Yeah."

"And then they came back."

"Maybe," he said. "maybe when I was . . . asleep." He looked sheepish.

"What did they have with them?"

"Some tools," Davis said. "Pickaxes, shovels, stuff like that . . ."

"They say what they were going to do?"

"No, I just told them they hadda leave."

"Okay, Ike," Clint said.

"You believe me?"

"I do."

"Can I get my job back?"

"Maybe," Clint said. "Do you want it back, after the way they treated you?"

"I need a job," Davis said. "A job's a job."

"Okay, then," Clint said. "But I need one more thing from you."

"What's that?"

"I need the names of the two men."

Davis worried his lower lip again. He went to drink some coffee, but the mug was empty. He set it down, then worked his hands nervously.

"Whatta you gonna do?"

"Check into it," Clint said. "Find out if they were the ones who sabotaged the shaft."

"And then what?"

"Find out who they work for."

"And go to the law?"

"The way I understand it," Clint said, "that wouldn't do any good."

"The sheriff's okay."

"I guess that will depend on who the two men work for, won't it, Ike?" Clint asked.

"Look . . ." Davis said nervously. "I don't wanna get nobody in trouble."

"As a night watchman, you might have to get somebody in trouble, Ike," Clint said. "Or lose your job . . . again. Understand?"

Davis hesitated, then nodded, and said, "Yeah, yeah, I understand."

"Okay, then," Clint said. "Why don't you pour me another cup of coffee and then tell me who the two men were, and who they work for."

SIX

When Clint went back to the mining office, the door was unlocked and Ben Blanchard was inside.

As he entered, he asked, "Where's Mahoney?"

"He's at the site. Did you talk to Ike?"

"I did," Clint said. "Mahoney led me to believe he was the town drunk. He says he had a couple of drinks, that's all. Fell asleep because he's been working three jobs."

"That's probably true."

Clint sat across from Blanchard.

"He talked to me, told me what he saw," Clint said. "I told him you'd give him his job back."

"Does he want it back? After the way we fired him?"

"He needs a job."

"Yeah, okay."

"With a raise."

"A raise?"

Clint nodded. "A raise."

Blanchard opened a drawer, took out a bottle of whiskey

and two glasses. He filled them both, then pushed one to Clint's side of the desk.

"Okay, then," he said. "What did he tell you?"

Dennis Mahoney looked down into shaft number one. The men had done a good job of digging it out partway.

"We gotta go faster, Joe," he told the man standing next to him.

"We're goin' as fast as we can, boss," Joe Lester said.

"Go faster, Joe," Mahoney said. "I want this shaft back the way it was by tomorrow."

"And what do we do if somebody caves it in again?" Lester asked.

"That ain't gonna happen, Joe," Mahoney said. "The boss brought somebody in to make sure of that."

"Who?"

"You'll find that out when the time is right," Mahoney said. "Just keep these men diggin'."

"Yeah, sure, boss," Lester said. "I'll do that."

Lester walked away, joined a group of men who were standing off to one side. He started talking to them, and they all began to nod.

Dennis Mahoney turned and started back toward town.

"Nick Cordell and Wes Underwood?" Blanchard repeated.

"Those are the names he gave me."

Blanchard frowned.

"Do you know those names?"

"I can't say I do," Blanchard said. "Who are they?"

"They work at a ranch called the Lazy K."

"The Lazy—that's Avery Kendall's ranch."

"That's what Davis told me."

"That sonofabitch!" Blanchard said. "Jesus Christ, you've been here five minutes and you already proved that Kendall has been behind the sabotage."

"Not quite."

"What do you mean?"

"Just because the two men were seen last night doesn't mean they did it," Clint said. "And if they did, just because they work for Kendall doesn't mean he was behind it."

"What are you talking about?"

"I'm talking about how the law would see it."

"The law? I don't need the law, Clint, I have you."

"And what do you think I can do with this information?" Clint asked.

"Make them talk!" Blanchard said. "Threaten them. Scare them! Christ, you're the Gunsmith, aren't you?"

"I don't use my reputation to frighten people," Clint said. "If you think that, Ben, then you don't know me at all."

"Okay, wait a minute," Blanchard said. He sat back in his chair and took a deep breath. "I'm sorry. I didn't mean to say that. I'm just . . . really upset."

"I can see that."

"Of course, you're right," Blanchard said. "Right now there's no proof."

"No, there isn't."

"So . . . what do we do now?"

"Well, you're right about one thing," Clint said. "I do have to talk to these two men, see what they have to say."

"Do you trust what Ike Davis told you?"

"I do."

"Then I guess you better tell him to come to work tomorrow."

"I will," Clint said. "Has Mahoney hired anybody else yet?"

"Not that I've heard."

"You're going to need two men on watch," Clint said.

"I know," Blanchard said. "I'll see that it gets done."

"Okay." Clint stood up."

"When will you talk to them?" Blanchard asked.

"I've only just arrived in town, Ben," Clint said. "Let me get my bearings. I'll probably do it tomorrow."

"But it's still pretty clear—uh, okay, tomorrow will do, then," Blanchard said. "I appreciate your help, Clint."

"Why don't we meet in the saloon tonight for a drink?" Clint asked.

"Which one?"

"You pick."

"The Dancing Lady," Blanchard said. "It's where I usually do my drinking."

"Okay," Clint said, "the Dancing Lady. I'll see you there. Maybe Mahoney, too."

"Okay."

Clint started for the door, then stopped and turned.

"You vouch for Mahoney, right?"

"I do," Blanchard said. "I brought him out here from back East. He's a good man. Why?"

"He was pretty quick to brand Davis a drunk and fire him without even hearing his story."

"Well . . . everybody makes mistakes," Blanchard said.

"Which is exactly why you're giving Ike Davis his job back, right?"

"Right," Blanchard agreed.

SEVEN

Clint left the mining office, shaking his head. He had to start thinking twice—and maybe three times—before responding to calls for help from friends.

He'd dealt with enough rich men to know how this was going to go. This Avery Kendall would use some of his employees to get his way, and when he couldn't, he'd import some hired guns. Maybe Clint's advice to Blanchard should be to sell out and get out of town. Yeah, make some money on your strike and get out. Let somebody else do the work, digging the salt out of the ground.

Walking back toward his hotel, he passed the Dancing Lady and decided to go in. Immediately, he saw the reason for the name. Above the bar was a painting of a dancing lady, only unlike most of the paintings you saw in Western saloons, this lady had clothes on. It looked to Clint like she was dancing ballet. He'd seen one or two ballets while in New York.

The place was about half full, no girls working the floor

yet, but they'd be out later. The place was too big not to have girls, and while the gaming tables were covered, they'd be in use later on with cowboys looking to impress the ladies.

He went to the bar and waved at the beefy bartender.

"Whataya want?" the man asked.

"Beer."

"Comin' up."

He drew a frothy beer, set it down in front of Clint.

"New in town?"

"Brand new."

"Wouldn't be the Gunsmith, would ya?"

"Why do you ask?"

The man shrugged his wide shoulders.

"Heard he was in town," the bartender said. "If you ain't him, no harm done."

"Yeah, well, I'm him."

"Beer's on the house."

"Why's that?"

"I've worked in saloons all around the West," the man said. "I comped beers to Wyatt Earp, Doc Holliday, Bat Masterson, Neil Brown, Bill Tilghman, Ben Allison . . . and some more I cain't remember now."

"That's quite a list."

"Yeah, but I never did get to serve the one I wanted."

"Let me guess," Clint said. "Hickok."

"You got it. Did you know 'im?"

"He was a good friend of mine."

"Then when you finish that one," the bartender said, "you can have his, also on the house. My name's Mike, by the way."

"Much obliged, Mike," Clint said.

"My pleasure. I got another customer."

"You willing to talk to me about this town?" Clint asked.

"Why not?"

"Come on back, then."

"Sure."

The bartender moved down the bar to serve two other customers. Clint sipped his beer, looked over his shoulder at the room. A few men seemed to find him interesting, but the bartender had explained that. Word had gotten around that he was in town. That was another good reason for him to leave town, but he had already promised Blanchard that he'd stay and help.

The bartender came back, slung his bar rag over his shoulder, and asked, "What's on your mind?"

"Fella named Avery Kendall."

"What about him?"

"That's what I want to know," Clint said. "Anything unusual about him?"

The bartender shrugged and said, "He's a rich man. What can I tell you? He thinks that money entitles him to anything he wants. And maybe it does."

"Does he employ guns?"

"Not at the moment," the man said, "but he has, and he probably will again. This about the salt mine?"

"Yep. You know Blanchard?"

"He drinks in here," the barkeep said. "Seems like an okay guy. I thought he was a flim-flam artist when he got to town, but then he struck salt."

"And that changed him?"

"Seemed to," the bartender said. "He stopped tryin' to sell people stuff, started working on his mine. Didn't offer anybody a piece of it either."

"So he's been straight since then."

"Well, I wouldn't know that," the bartender said. "I just don't think he's been tryin' to flim-flam anybody that I know of."

"Well, that's good to know anyway."

"You gonna help Blanchard with his problems?"

"He's a friend of mine, so yeah, I'm going to help him," Clint said. "What do you know about it?"

"Just what I hear," the bartender said, "which is the same thing everybody else hears. He's having trouble. Wait. You think Kendall is behind it?"

"Is anybody else in town interested in taking over his salt mine?"

"I wouldn't think so," the bartender said. "Naw, nobody else has got the money . . . I got another customer. Anything else?"

"No," Clint said, "not until I'm ready for that second beer."

"Just gimme a wave."

"I'll do that."

EIGHT

Clint was working on that second beer when the sheriff came through the batwings.

"Well, well," the lawman said, "I was just doin' my rounds and look who I run into. How are things, Mr. Adams?"

Clint had a feeling the man had been rehearsing his lines. He was doing everything he could not to appear nervous.

"Buy you a beer, Sheriff Cade?" Clint asked.

"Don't mind if I do."

The sheriff bellied up to the bar and Clint waved at the bartender.

"Thanks, Mike," Cade said when the bartender set the beer down in front of him. "What've you been up to, Mr. Adams?"

"Just staying out of trouble, Sheriff," Clint said. "I think that's what you wanted me to do."

"That's exactly what I wanted you to do."

"Well, there you go." Clint looked around. "This is a pretty nice saloon. You drink here a lot?"

"I don't drink anywhere a lot," Cade said. "Just a beer

every once in a while. But this is better than most." As if to illustrate his point, he put his mug down on the bar, only half finished. "Gotta get back to work. Thanks for the beer."

Cade left and Clint finished his own beer before paying for Cade's and leaving the saloon himself.

When Mahoney returned to the office, Blanchard told him what Clint had said.

"What?" Mahoney said. "Rehire Ike Davis? No, I won't!"

"I already told Clint we would."

"Ben, do you know how that will make me look in front of my men?" Mahoney argued. "I can't be rehiring a man the day after I fired him."

"Dennis, damn it," Blanchard said. "I told Clint we would."

"Why does Adams believe what Davis told him? I told you, the man was drunk."

"Did you ask him what he saw?"

"No," Mahoney said, "because he couldn't see a thing. He . . . was . . . drunk!"

"Clint doesn't think so."

"Look, Ben, I know you put a lot of stock in Adams," Mahoney said, "but he didn't see Davis that night, I did."

"Look," Blanchard said, "if Davis's information turns out to be wrong, you can fire him again."

"Oh, that's great," the foreman said. "Firing a guy, hiring him back, and then firing him again, that's going to make me look real strong to the men."

"Look," Blanchard said, "the men know you're strong, they know you're the foreman. They know what you say goes—"

"Except in this case."

"Yes," Blanchard said, "except in this one case. Dennis,

Clint's been here less than a day and already he's come up with something."

"Two names, of men who work for Kendall. We could've guessed that."

"That they work for Kendall, yes," Blanchard said, "but not their names. He got that."

"From Ike Davis," Mahoney said, "who probably made up the names to get his job back."

"Okay," Blanchard said, "okay. How's this? I won't hire Davis back until we've checked out his story."

Mahoney subsided for a moment, then said, "That's better. You'll see, his story won't check out. Hiring him back would be a mistake."

Blanchard drywashed his face with both hands.

"We'll see," he said. "Clint's going to talk to the men tomorrow."

"Tomorrow?" Mahoney said. "Why wait until tomorrow? If his information is so good, why not do it today?"

"He just got to town today," Blanchard said. "He's got to get his bearings. Tomorrow's good enough. Meanwhile we need some night watchmen tonight. If I'm not going to rehire Davis, you need to pick out two of the men to stand watch. Just until we can hire two new men."

"Yeah, okay," Mahoney said, "I'll get on that right now. I'll—I'll use Joe Lester and . . . and Fenmore."

"Yeah, okay," Blanchard said, "that sounds good."

"Yeah," Mahoney said, "good. Look, Dennis, are you sure you don't want to fire me and make Adams your foreman? I mean, he is a legend—"

"Don't be stupid!" Blanchard said, cutting the foreman off. "You're the foreman, he's my friend. He's here to help, that's all."

"Yeah, okay," Mahoney said. "I'll go and talk to Joe and Fenmore."

"Okay."

Mahoney turned and left the office. Blanchard sat back in his chair and heaved a huge sigh. What a mess, he thought. Maybe he should just sell out to Kendall and get out of town. But then the rich man would win, and Blanchard didn't like the sound of that. He didn't want the rich man to win.

Not until he was the rich man.

NINE

Clint remained in his room for most of the afternoon and returned to the Dancing Lady after a steak supper.

The saloon was in full swing, crowded to the rafters with customers drinking and gambling and groping the saloon girls as they went by.

He went to the bar, managed to elbow a place for himself. A couple of cowboys turned to give him hard look, but when they saw who he was, they gave him space.

"Hey, you're back," Mike the bartender said.

"And I'll pay for my beer this time," Clint said.

"No argument here," Mike said. He set another frothy one in front of Clint.

"Have you seen Ben Blanchard?" Clint asked.

"Not so far, but when he does come in, it's usually late," Mike said. "After eight. I think he works 'til then."

"Probably," Clint said.

"Why not take a chance on a game of chance while you wait?" Mike offered.

"No, not tonight," Clint said. "I think I'll just nurse my beer and wait."

"Suit yourself."

Clint nodded and Mike went to serve other thirsty customers.

Clint turned with his beer in his hand and looked the room over. Poker, faro, and a roulette wheel, and players were three deep. There were four girls working the floor, wearing red, green, blue, and purple dresses. They were easier to tell apart that way since three of them were blond, and the fourth was dark-haired.

The dark-haired girl looked over at him, smiled, and walked toward him. She was wearing the blue dress and filled it out nicely. Her creamy bosom overflowed from it.

"Are you the Gunsmith?" she asked.

"Guilty."

"I thought so," she said. "I heard you were in town."

"Seems like everybody's heard that."

"That's what happens when you're a famous man," she told him.

"What's your name?"

"Sarah."

"Sarah," he said, "you can call me Clint."

"Okay, Clint," she said. "Stick around. Don't go anywhere."

"I'll be around for a while," he promised.

"Don't let any of these other girls steal you away from me," she said, touching his chest with her index finger.

"I won't."

She turned and went back to work.

* * *

A few minutes before eight o'clock, Ben Blanchard came through the batwings. Clint had just gotten a second beer, having nursed the first one until it was warm.

"One for your friend?" Mike asked.

"Hang on," Clint said. "I'm not sure if he'll want a beer, or whiskey."

Blanchard joined Clint at the bar and said, "A beer will be fine."

"Beer, Mike," Clint said.

"Comin' up."

"You made a friend already?" Blanchard asked.

Clint's eyes went to Sarah, winding her way between tables, and said, "You don't know the half of it."

Blanchard followed his friend's gaze, laughed, and said, "I can guess."

They both turned and leaned on the bar.

"You talk to Mahoney about Ike Davis?"

"Yeah," Blanchard said. "He's not happy."

"He thinks I'm undermining his authority, huh?"

"Exactly."

"I can see that," Clint said. "I hope he won't take it too personally."

"I'll try to calm him down," Blanchard said. "I, uh, I did tell him I wouldn't hire Davis back until we find out if his information is good."

"I guess that's fair. What about night watchmen tonight?"

"He's going to pull two of our men out and have them watch," Blanchard said.

"That sounds good."

"I tell you," Blanchard said, "I don't know how much more of this I can take."

"Thinking of giving up?" Clint asked.

"The thought had occurred to me," Blanchard said, "but I can't do it. I just can't let Kendall win."

"Okay, then," Clint said. "So we'll agree to do what we've got to do."

"Yes."

"All of us?"

"Yes," Blanchard said. "Dennis will come around. I'll see to it."

"I'm not looking for his job," Clint said. "He's got to understand that."

"He will," Blanchard said.

"Then we'll figure this out."

"I'll drink to that."

The two men clinked glasses.

TEN

When Clint undid the back of Sarah's dress, those creamy breasts just fell out.

"I know," she said, "I'm too big, like a goddamned cow."

"Not at all," he said, taking a breast in each hand. "I love big breasts. Gives a man something to hold on to. And something to bite into."

She laughed as he lifted them to his mouth.

"That's what I was hoping you'd say," she told him. "I was hoping one of those skinny blondes wouldn't catch your eye."

"Not a chance," he said. "Not with you in the room."

With her hair down, it hung past her shoulders. He tugged the dress the rest of the way down so she could step out of it. She had wide hips, a full butt, heavy thighs, and solid legs. Everything a man could ask for in his bed.

"Now you," she said, reaching for his clothes.

His gun belt was already hanging on the bedpost, so she undid his belt and tugged his pants down. His already hard cock sprang out at attention.

"Oh, yes," she said.

She took his hard penis in both hands, caressed it, stroked it, kissed it, and finally took it into her mouth. The sucking of her mouth brought him up onto his toes.

She sucked him for a while like that, wetting him thoroughly, and then he withdrew from her mouth and pushed her down onto her back.

He put his hands back on her breasts, squeezing them and rubbing the nipples with his thumbs. She moaned and put her hands up over her head, stretching. As he leaned over her and worked on her big tits with his hands, his hard cock rubbed over her thick black pubic bush. Her pussy started to get wet and she began to move her hips, rubbing her wetness against him.

Almost by itself, his cock suddenly slid into her . . .

Mahoney had found his two men, Joe Lester and Will Fenmore, sitting around a fire near the bunkhouse, eating a plate of beans each. They didn't like it when he told them they'd be on watch that night, but they both wanted to keep their jobs, so they didn't argue.

Now they were on watch together, mostly keeping an eye on the number one shaft, the main source of salt until they were able to sink another shaft that would yield the same amount.

They each held a rifle, and neither of them wore a handgun. Joe Lester was afraid he'd shoot himself in the foot, and Fenmore just didn't own one.

"What are we supposed to do if we see somebody?" Fenmore asked.

"Chase 'em off, I guess."

"How?"

"By shootin' at 'em!"

"What if we hit 'em?"

"They shouldn't be sneakin' around the mine, Fenmore," Lester said.

"Yeah, but I didn't sign on here to be shootin' anybody," Fenmore argued.

"Then shoot over their heads," Joe Lester said. "We only wanna run 'em off."

"Okay, okay," Fenmore said, "I can do that. I ain't such a good shot anyway."

"Now you tell me."

"Besides, what happened to the night watchman?"

"Ike Davis got fired for bein' asleep on the job when the shaft fell in."

"Well then," Fenmore said, "we better make sure we keep each other awake, because I don't wanna lose my job."

"Me neither," Lester said. "So guess we better just keep on talkin'."

"About what?"

"I dunno . . . hey, did you see that new Chinese whore at the cathouse?"

Dennis Mahoney was with the new Chinese whore at that moment. He'd never been with a Chinese woman before, and when he heard about this one, he was first in line. Now he made a habit of using her.

Her name was Soon Li. She didn't like Mahoney, but she wasn't paid to like the men she had to lie down with. She only had to please them.

After the first time with him, she learned what he liked, and how to finish him quickly. She used her mouth and her hands to make him come fast.

"Oh wow," he said, "that was fantastic."

Yes, she thought, now he thinks he is a real man. This one did not belong in the West. He would soon find that out.

She rolled over, not bothering to cover her nudity. Her small breasts were tipped with dark brown nipples, and the hair at the apex of her thighs was very black.

"You were very tense," she said.

"Yes," he said, "things are very . . . bad at work."

She studied him. He was a soft man, both physically and mentally. She watched him get dressed, covering his soft body with his clothes, and felt nothing but disgust.

He left money on the dresser and left the room.

Ben Blanchard sat in his armchair in his house, a glass of whiskey in his hand. He was going to finish it, and then go to the mine. It was his; he should be the one guarding it, not two of his employees.

But when he finished the drink, he picked up the bottle and poured another . . .

Clint fucked Sarah hard.

She wanted it that way, imploring him on, and he was happy to oblige her.

Her skin was flushed, her eyes glazed, her lips swollen. She wrapped powerful legs around him, encircled him with her arms, and pulled him to her. She bit into his shoulder, raked his back with her nails.

He didn't feel any of it. All he felt was what was happening between his legs. His release was building up in his legs, And when it came exploding out of him, he bellowed like a rutting bull . . .

ELEVEN

"Who's that?" Fenmore asked.

"How the fuck do I know?" Joe Lester asked. "Besides, I don't hear nothin'."

"Over there," Fenmore said, pointing his rifle, his finger tensing on the trigger.

"Don't start shootin' at shadows, Fenmore," Lester warned.

"Hey, you guys," a voice called.

"Jesus," Lester said, "don't shoot. It's the boss."

Dennis Mahoney appeared from out of the darkness. He had come directly from the whorehouse.

"Anything?" he asked.

"Nothin' until you got here, boss," Lester said.

"Okay, well, I'm going to stay here awhile with you fellas," Mahoney said.

"That mean we can leave?" Fenmore asked hopefully.

"I said with you, not instead of you," Mahoney said.

"You ain't got a gun, boss," Lester said.

"I never carry a gun."

"Maybe you oughtta start," Lester said. "There's probably one in the office."

"Okay," Mahoney said, "I'll go and have a look."

Clint told Sarah she could stay in his hotel room. "I'll be back."

"Where are you going?"

"There's just something I have to take care of," he said, strapping on his gun.

She pushed the sheet down to her waist so he could see her big breasts. Her pink nipples were still hard, puckered.

"Come back soon," she said.

"I will."

He forced himself to walk out the door.

Clint left the hotel and walked to the mine office. It was dark and locked. Blanchard had told him where the mine was, outside of town. Not too far to walk, but it was dark. He'd probably get lost.

He walked to the livery, found that it was also locked. Eclipse was inside. He could have broken in, but was it necessary? Blanchard had told him he'd have two men on watch at the mine tonight. He should probably just let them do their job. In the morning he'd find the two men who worked for Avery Kendall and talk to them.

He decided to just go back to his room, where he had a warm woman waiting for him in a warm bed.

He woke the next morning with his cock in Sarah's mouth. She was sucking him avidly, wetly, making slurping noises that he found only increased his excitement. He reached down to hold her head lightly as it bobbed up and down on him, faster and faster, one hand holding him at the base, the other fondling his testicles.

When he exploded into her mouth, he was sure the entire town must have heard him . . .

"You gonna be stayin' in town awhile?" she asked as she got dressed.

"A few days at least," he said, watching her.

"Good," she said. "I'm not done with you yet."

"Well," he said, "I sure as hell am not done with you either, lady."

Her breasts and butt disappeared beneath her clothes and then she leaned over to kiss him. He grabbed her and held her so that the kiss went on a long time.

"Bastard," she whispered against his mouth. "I have to go now."

"Come back to bed."

"Tonight."

"We could all be dead tonight."

She straightened and stared down at him.

"What's that mean?"

"Just that we should grab what we can while we can."

"Do you know somethin'—"

"I don't know anything," he said. "I was just trying to get you to come back to bed."

"You are a bastard, aren't you?" she said. "Come by the saloon tonight."

"Okay."

"And then, when I finish work, we can come back here."

"That suits me."

"Maybe," she said, "I can convince one of my girlfriends to come with us."

"Really?"

She slapped his face lightly and said, "Gotcha," and left.

After Sarah was gone, he got up, washed and dressed, and went down to find some breakfast. The hotel had a small dining room, so he decided to try it. If it was good, it would come in handy.

"Steak and eggs," he told the waiter.

"Comin' up."

"And coffee, strong."

"Only kind we serve."

It turned out he was right. The coffee was good, and it was strong. When the waiter brought the steak, it was cooked perfectly. And he brought a basket of biscuits, hot.

Clint was tucking into it all when Dennis Mahoney walked in. He looked like he'd been up all night.

"The desk clerk told me you were in here," he said.

"Sit," Clint said. "You look like you could use some coffee."

"You're right."

Clint waved to the waiter for another cup. When he brought it, he said, "And bring my friend the same thing I'm having."

Mahoney didn't argue. Clint poured him some coffee from the pot, and went back to eating.

"Ben told me you're going to question the two men from the Kendall ranch today."

"That's right."

"I want to go with you."

Clint studied him, then said, "All right."

"No argument?"

"No argument."

The waiter brought a platter for Mahoney, and he started eating.

TWELVE

Clint walked with Mahoney to the livery to saddle Eclipse.

"You got a horse?" he asked Mahoney.

"What? No."

"Can you ride?"

"I can ride."

"Okay," Clint said, "while I saddle mine, you better rent one."

"Yeah, okay."

As Mahoney started to walk away, Clint said, "Hey, you know the way to the ranch?"

"I know it."

"Okay, good," Clint said. "Get that horse."

Mahoney rented a gentle-looking mare, good enough for the ride to the ranch. Not much good for anything else.

"How'd it go last night?" Clint asked.

"No problems," Mahoney said. "I had two men on watch, I stood with them for a while."

"Looks to me like you stayed with them all night," Clint said.

"Yeah, well, I feel responsible."

"That's what makes you a good foreman," Clint said. "You know, Mahoney, I'm not after your job. I'm just trying to help a friend."

"I get it," Mahoney said. "I really do. I just don't like having my authority questioned. It doesn't make me look good in front of the men."

"And I get that," Clint said. "I'll try not to do it . . ."

Mahoney looked at him.

"Again," he finished. "I'll try not to do it again."

"Well, we're not hiring Ike Davis back unless his information checks out," Mahoney said.

"Right. How far is this ranch?"

"It'll take us another twenty minutes or so," Mahoney said. "Or maybe, on this horse, a little longer."

"That's okay," Clint said. "We're not in a hurry."

When they reached the ranch, Clint wasn't impressed. It didn't look like the operation of a rich man. One-story house, not very big, a corral and a barn. A few men milling about.

"You sure this is the place?"

"This is it."

"It's not much."

"Maybe that's how he stays rich," Mahoney said, "by not spending a lot of money on equipment."

They rode up to the house, attracting the attention of the few hands who were around.

"Wait," Clint said as they dismounted. "Does Kendall live here?"

"No, he lives in town."

"Now you tell me," Clint said. "We could have started with him."

"I thought you wanted to talk to his two men first," Mahoney said.

"Yeah, okay," Clint said, "we can do it that way."

Clint looked around. While a few men were eyeing them, nobody was coming over to see who they were, or to try and help.

And nobody came out of the house.

"I guess we better knock."

They approached the door and Clint knocked. He was surprised when the door was answered by a handsome-looking woman in her forties, with long dark hair.

"Can I help you?" she asked.

"My name is Clint Adams," Clint said. "Are you Mrs. Kendall?"

She laughed.

"No, no, my name's Kitty Lane," she said. "I work for Mr. Kendall."

"Doing what, if I may ask?"

"Running this place," she said, "and if I may ask, why are you asking? And who's your friend?"

"Oh, sorry," Clint said, "this is Dennis Mahoney. He's the foreman at the King Street Mine."

"Oh, yes," Kitty said. "The mine. And you? Why is the Gunsmith interested in mining?"

"The owner is a friend of mine," he said. "Can we come inside?"

"Sure, why not?"

She led them to a small living room. The house looked much better inside, where it showed a woman's touch.

"What can I do for you gents?"

"We're looking for two of your men," Clint said.

"Which two?"

"Nick Cordell and Wes Underwood."

"Oh, them."

"What about them?" Clint asked.

"I fired them."

"When?"

"Earlier today."

"Wow," Clint said. "That must have been the first thing you did this morning after breakfast."

"Before."

"Why'd you fire them?"

"They disappeared a couple of days ago. Came back as if nothing had happened. I sent them packing."

"You have that authority?"

"I do."

"They must have had some belongings in the bunkhouse, right?"

"Sure."

"Could they still be packing?"

"They better be gone by now," she said, "but I'll take you over to the bunkhouse."

"Thank you."

"Just give me a minute to clean up."

"You look pretty clean to me," Clint said.

Kitty smiled. "You're sweet. I'll be right back." She went to the door of what he presumed was her bedroom, turned, and said, "Don't go away."

They left the house and followed the shapely Kitty to the bunkhouse.

"It should be empty now. The men are at work."

They entered, found it as empty as she predicted it would be.

"Those two were theirs." She pointed to two bunks where the thin mattresses had been rolled up. "I'm going to have to replace them."

They went back outside.

"Why did you need to speak to them?"

"There was some sabotage at the mine two nights ago," Clint said. "Those two men were seen there."

"So that's what they were doing when they were supposed to be working here?" she said, arching one eyebrow. "I'm glad I fired them."

"You have any idea which way they rode when they left?" Clint asked.

"Sorry, no," she said. "Would you like to come back inside for a cool drink?"

"I don't think so," Clint said. "I want to see if I can track them down. Thanks for your help."

They walked back to the house, where Clint and Mahoney mounted up.

"By the way," Clint said to her, "when I see your boss, I'll tell him what a fine job you're doing."

"You're going to talk to Mr. Kendall?"

"As soon as I get back to town," Clint said. "After all, if these men did sabotage the mine, they did it while working for him."

"That doesn't mean he had any knowledge of it," she said.

"Doesn't mean he didn't." He touched the brim of his hat politely. "Have a good day."

They turned their horses and rode off.

Clint spent some time trying to pick up the trail of two horses, but with no luck.

"Where would they go?" Mahoney asked.

"Where would you go if you suddenly got fired?" Clint asked him.

"A saloon."

"There you go," Clint said. "Let's head back to town."

They rode back into town and discussed their options.

"We don't know what they look like," Mahoney said.

"But Ike Davis does," Clint said. "We can take him with us as we canvas the saloons in town."

"If that's what you want to do," Mahoney said, shaking his head.

"But first," Clint said, "let's talk to Mr. Kendall. Where would he be?"

"Either in his office, or his club."

"Club?" Clint asked. "You mean . . . like a cattlemen's club?"

"Yeah, only it isn't. It's just . . . a club." He shrugged. "A men's club? I don't know what else to call it. The rich men in the area go there to drink, and eat and do whatever else they want to do."

"Whores?" Clint asked.

"Probably."

"Hmm . . ."

"What are you thinking?"

"That we might have another way of getting some information," Clint said. "Take me to that club and let's start there."

"Okay," Mahoney said. "This way."

THIRTEEN

The club looked like it used to be a hotel.

They stepped to the front door, but found their way blocked by a beefy man, who folded his arms. Clint noticed that he wasn't armed.

"This is a private club."

"I need to speak to one of your members," Clint said. "Avery Kendall. Is he inside?"

"I ain't seen him this morning."

"Are you sure?"

"I know what Mr. Kendall looks like," the man said. "He's our richest member."

"Okay," Clint said, "then I guess we'd better go over and check his office."

"If he ain't here," the man said, "he's probably over there."

"Could he be eating somewhere?"

"He only eats here."

"Okay, then," Clint said. "Thanks."

They turned to leave, and then Clint turned back.

"How do you stop somebody from getting in if they really want to get in, and they have a gun?"

The man smiled.

"I make 'em eat it."

Mahoney led Clint to a large brick building.

"This looks like City Hall," Clint commented.

"Nope," Mahoney said, "just Mr. Kendall's building. It's the newest structure in town."

"Impressive."

"He has lots of money," Mahoney said. "Lots."

"And I assume he does business outside of Hutchinson? And outside of Kansas?"

"Oh, yes," Mahoney said. "His holdings are far-reaching."

They stepped to the door and tried the handle. It opened, and no one was there to block their way.

They found themselves in an entry hall, with doors all around them.

"Why all the offices?" Clint asked.

Mahoney shrugged.

"All I know is Kendall's is upstairs in the front, where he can see the street."

"Okay," Clint said, "upstairs it is."

They went up, turned, and saw a door that said AVERY KENDALL on it. That was all, just his name.

They stepped to the door, looked at each other, and knocked.

"Do you know him?" Clint asked quickly.

"We've met, but I don't know if he'll remember."

A man's voice yelled, "Come!"

Clint opened the door and they stepped in.

"Mahoney, isn't it?" the man behind the desk asked. "Who's your friend? Oh, wait a minute, don't tell. The Gunsmith, right? Clint Adams?"

Kendall was a tall, gray-haired man in an expensive suit, sitting behind an equally expensive desk.

"You're well informed," Clint said.

"You bet I am," Kendall said, "but him I know from the salt mine. I heard you were in town, heard you were friends with Ben Blanchard. If I can't put two and two together by now, I don't deserve to be as rich as I am. Come in, sit down. Can I offer you a drink? Some brandy?"

"Not for me," Mahoney said.

"None for me either," Clint said.

"Suit yourselves," Kendall said. "If I can't give you a drink, then what can I do for you?"

"You can answer a few questions."

"About what?"

"Two of your men."

"My men?"

"They work at your ranch."

"Oh," he said, "well, Kitty runs the ranch. Have you been out there?"

"We have," Clint said. "She told us she fired them."

"Well then, she did," Kendall said. "That's why I employ her, to do the hiring and firing—and she's good at it."

"We understand that," Clint said. "But . . . did you know the two men?"

"I don't even know what two men you're talking about."

"Nick Cordell and Wes Underwood," Clint said.

"Still don't know them," Kendall said. "What did they do?"

"You know what they did," Mahoney said. "They sabotaged our number one shaft, like you told them to."

"That's quite an accusation, Mr. Mahoney," Kendall said calmly. "Why don't you take it to the sheriff?"

"You know why," Mahoney said. "The sheriff is firmly in your pocket."

"Then go to the mayor, if that's what you think."

"There's room in your pocket for him, too," Mahoney said.

Kendall looked at Clint.

"If you listen to Mr. Mahoney," he said, "you would think I had everybody in my pockets. That would give me very big pockets."

"Deep," Clint said.

"Excuse me?"

"What he's saying is you have deep pockets."

"If that's a reference to my money," the man said, "I have worked very hard to have deep pockets. I'm not going to apologize for it."

"We're not asking you to," Clint said. "We're just asking you—telling you—go keep the money in your pockets when it comes to the King Street Mine."

"Or what, Mr. Adams?" Kendall asked. "You'll shoot me down in the street? I'm afraid the days of solving your problems that way are gone. The Old West is dead, sir. And you are an anachronism."

"Talk about an anachronism," Clint said. "How about the rich man in town who tries to own everything?"

Kendall smiled and said, "Money never gets old, Mr. Adams."

"Maybe not," Clint said, "but you'll find it hard to spend in prison."

"Or dead," Mahoney added.

Clint gave him an annoyed look.

"I think it's time for you both to leave," Kendall said.

"You may have sent those two men away, Mr. Kendall," Clint said, "but I'm going to find them, and they'll testify that you paid them to sabotage the mine."

"I wish you good luck with that, Mr. Adams," Kendall said.

"Come on," Clint said to Mahoney.

FOURTEEN

Outside the building they stopped on the boardwalk.

"I could have throttled him," Mahoney said.

"That wouldn't have accomplished anything," Clint told him. "You would have had to kill him."

Mahoney opened his mouth to answer, but closed it again. He hesitated and then said, "I couldn't have done that."

"Don't worry," Clint said. "It's not an easy thing to kill a man."

"But . . . you do it all the time."

"I've done it a lot," Clint said, "from necessity. And it's never been easy."

"I'm sorry," Mahoney said, "I didn't mean—"

"Forget it," Clint said. "Let's go and tell Ben what we've found out."

"Which is?"

"Not a whole lot."

* * *

As they entered the office, Ben Blanchard looked up from his desk.

"Anything?" he asked.

"Nothing," Mahoney said.

Blanchard looked at Clint, who sat down across from his friend and told him about the morning's events.

"Well," Blanchard said, looking on the bright side, "I think that pretty much confirms that those two men—Cordell and Underwood?—are guilty. Kendall got them out of town pretty quick, probably with money in their pockets."

"We figured they'd probably head for a saloon if they really got fired," Mahoney said.

"But if it was phony," Clint said, "maybe they'll just head for another town."

"Can you find them?" Blanchard asked. "If we can get them to testify, we'll have something on Kendall. And there won't be anything the sheriff can do about it."

"We had a problem picking up their trail," Clint said. "There are a lot of tracks around the ranch."

"So you can't track them?"

"No."

"Maybe there's somebody in town who can."

"You got an idea?" Clint asked.

"No," Blanchard said. "I don't have that kind of knowledge."

"We might just have to check the closest towns," Clint said.

"That'll take a while," Blanchard said. "What do we do in the meantime?"

"Keep mining," Clint said, "and hire yourself two night watchmen."

"One," Mahoney said.

"What?" Blanchard asked.

"We're hiring Ike Davis back, so we only need one more man."

"You're convinced Davis was right?" Blanchard asked.

"I am."

"Then you better go and give him his job back," Blanchard said. "And find us a second man."

"I'll get on that right away," Mahoney said.

"And make sure you get some rest," Clint said. "You're not going to do anybody any good if you're out on your feet."

Mahoney waved, nodded, and left the office.

"He was up all night," Clint told Blanchard.

"I told you he's a good man."

"Seems you were right," Clint said. "Look, I'm going to ask around town for a tracker. If I find one, you'll have to pay him."

"I'll pay him," Blanchard said. "You find him, you hire him, and I'll pay him."

FIFTEEN

Clint figured he couldn't ask the sheriff about a tracker in town, so he decided he'd go to someone even better. The people who knew everything about everybody in a town were the bartenders.

Clint walked to the Dancing Lady and entered. At that time of day, Mike the bartender was cleaning glasses behind the bar.

"Hey," Mike said, "beer?"

"Beer," Clint said, "and information."

"I got both," Mike said. He drew the beer, set it in front of Clint, and said, "That's one. What's the other?"

"I need a tracker," Clint said. "I figure every town's got at least one."

"A tracker."

"Somebody I can pay," Clint said, "and trust."

"Ah," Mike said, "I know just the guy."

"Good. Where do I find him?"

Mike looked past Clint and said, "Right back there."

Clint turned. The man Mike was indicating sat at a table alone, with a bottle of whiskey and a glass. At the moment, his head was down on the table.

"Him?" Clint asked. "He's drunk."

"He's always drunk," Mike said. "He was sitting there last night, only you couldn't see him."

"Mike, what good is he to me if he's always drunk?" Clint asked.

"He's always drunk," Mike said, "except when he's working."

"He can stay off the whiskey while he's working?"

"Yes."

"How does he manage that?"

"Because if he's working for you, he knows you're gonna pay him money he can use to buy more whiskey."

"And he stays sober until then?"

"Yes."

"Are you sure?"

"I am," Mike said, "if you don't pay him until the job is done."

Clint looked again at the man, who hadn't moved.

"Okay," he said, "what's his name?"

"Haven," Mike said.

"First name? Last name?"

"Just Haven."

"Okay," Clint said, "thanks."

Clint grabbed his beer, started away, but then turned back.

"How much has he had to drink?"

"It doesn't matter," Mike said. "He only gets so drunk. Once he reaches that point, it doesn't matter how much more he drinks."

"Really?"

"Yep," Mike said. "He's the only man I've ever seen drink like that."

"Okay," Clint said, "okay. Thanks. Okay if I take my beer with me?"

"He won't mind."

Clint nodded and walked over to the table. Haven still didn't move.

"Haven?"

No answer.

"Haven!"

Nothing.

"Hey." He reached across and shook the man by the shoulder. "Haven!"

Haven sat straight up, his eyes wide. When he saw the whiskey bottle, he grabbed for it.

"Whoa," Clint said, grabbing it first.

"That's mine."

"You don't need it," Clint said. "I'm offering you a job."

"A job? Doing what?"

"Tracking."

Haven sat back. He was a dark man—dark hair, dark skin—in his thirties. He had about a week's growth of stubble on his face.

"Who or what am I tracking?" he asked, looking at Clint with bloodshot eyes.

"Two men," Clint said.

"What did they do?"

"I just want to talk to them first, but I think they committed an act of sabotage."

"How long have they been gone?"

"Since this morning."

"From where?" As he asked the questions, amazingly the man seemed to grow less and less drunk.

"From the Kendall ranch, outside of town."

"They work for Kendall?"

"They did."

"Do you work for him?"

"No," Clint said, "I'm acting in the interest of Ben Blanchard, of the King Street Salt Mine."

"And who's payin' me?"

"Blanchard."

Haven wiped his face, sat up straighter, and asked in a perfectly sober voice, "How much?"

"How much do you want?"

SIXTEEN

"This is Haven," Clint said, presenting the tracker to Ben Blanchard.

"Mr. Haven," Blanchard said. "Do you think you can help us?"

"According to what Mr. Adams says, yes, sir."

"Well, and how much will you be charging us for your services?"

"Mr. Blanchard, when we're done, you pay me what you think is fair."

"When we're done?"

"Yes, sir."

"No money before?" Blanchard looked from Haven to Clint and back again.

"No, sir," Haven said. "If that's all right."

"That's fine," Blanchard said. "When can you get started?"

Haven rubbed the stubble on his face and said, "I got to get cleaned up. In about an hour?"

"An hour will be fine."

"Thank you, sir."

"I'll meet you right back here, Haven," Clint said.

"Okay."

Haven left the office.

"Is he any good?" Blanchard asked.

"That's what I've been told," Clint said, "but he only has to be better than me."

"You taking anybody else with you?"

"Like who? Mahoney?" Clint asked. "He'd shoot himself in the foot. No, Haven and I will handle it. We'll find Cordell and Underwood and bring them back here."

"You do that," Blanchard said, "and we got Kendall."

"I hope so," Clint said.

"You going to wait for Haven here?"

"Might as well."

"Have a seat and some coffee, then."

"Don't mind if I do."

Hector Raines was in the saloon when Clint approached Haven's table. He heard the conversation, waited until both men had left the saloon, then got up and left himself. He hurried to Avery Kendall's building, climbed to the second floor, and knocked.

"Come!"

He went in.

"Hector," Kendall said. "What have you got for me?"

"The Gunsmith was just in the Dancing Lady, Mr. Kendall," Raines said, holding his hat in his hands.

"And?"

"He hired Haven."

Although he knew the answer, he asked, "To do what?"

"He wants him to track two men," Raines said. "I figured he was talkin' about Cordell and Underwood."

"And I'm sure you're right," Kendall said. "Have you seen my men Belmont or Ellis?"

"No, sir."

"Well, find one of them and tell him to get over here," Kendall said.

"Yes, sir."

Kendall took out a few bills and handed Hector Raines the money.

"Thank you, sir."

"Do it quick, Hector," Kendall said, "and I'll give you the same again."

"Yessir!"

The man hurried from the office, and the building.

Kendall sat back in his chair. Trying to kill the Gunsmith would be risky. There were a few other things he could try first, but if push came to shove, he was going to have to find the right man for the job.

SEVENTEEN

Haven came out of the barbershop, freshly shorn and bathed. He hadn't felt this clean in weeks. Now he needed to go to his room and pick up his gun. He never wore it unless he was working.

He had a small room over the hardware store, which they let him have for free as long as he swept up at the end of every day. This job did not stop him from drinking, as he did not consider it to be "work." Not the kind of work he really did anyway.

He walked to the store, climbed the stairs on the side, and entered the room. He opened the chest of drawers he had, drew out the gun belt with the worn Colt in it, and his Bowie knife. He strapped on the gun, then clipped the knife to his belt. But before doing that, he changed into clean clothes—the only other set of clothes he had. And finally he slipped off his boots and pulled on a pair of moccasins.

Now he was ready to do his new job.

* * *

"Yeah, I know Haven," Abe Ellis said to Kendall.

"Well, I want you to find him and make sure he can't leave town."

"How do you want me to do that, Mr. Kendall?" Ellis asked.

"I don't know. Hobble him. Break a leg. Shoot him."

"Kill 'im?"

Kendall hesitated, then said, "Only if there's no other way."

"Okay if I get some help?"

"As much as you want," Kendall said. "I'll pay you and you pay them."

"Okay."

Kendall took out an envelope and passed it to the man.

"Have you seen Belmont?"

"Not lately."

"Look," Kendall said, "Clint Adams is in town. If he gets in my way. I'll need somebody to take care of him."

"The Gunsmith? Geez, that's out of my league, Mr. Kendall," Ellis admitted.

"Well, do me a favor, will you? Find me Belmont, or somebody who doesn't think the Gunsmith is out of their league."

"Yessir, I'll sure do that. "When do you want Haven dealt with?"

"Right away."

"Yessir," Ellis said. "I'll get right on it."

"Good."

"I can be doing something better than just sitting here watching you do paperwork," Clint said to Blanchard.

"Like what?"

"I'll pick up a few supplies Haven and I will need," he said, standing up. "I don't know how long we'll be out there."

"Here." Blanchard opened his petty cash box and passed Clint some money. "I should cover that expense."

"No argument from me," Clint said, accepting the money. "I'll see you in a while. If Haven gets back before I do, sit on him."

"I will."

Clint nodded and left the office.

He was coming out of the mercantile, carrying a burlap sack, when he saw Haven on the other side of the street. The man seemed to be heading for the mining office. He was about to call out when he saw something else.

There were four men, wearing guns, walking toward Haven, and they seemed to be moving with bad intentions.

Clint stepped into the street.

EIGHTEEN

Abe Ellis saw Haven down the street and said to his men, "There he is. Now remember, we don't kill 'im unless we have to."

"How do we know if we have to?" one of them asked.

"If he forces our hand, you'll know." He looked at the other three men. "Anybody got a problem with killin' him?"

"Haven is harmless," one man said, "but if we gotta, we gotta."

"I'd kill anybody for money," another said. "I got no problem."

Ellis looked at the third man, who shook his head.

"Okay then," he said, "let's do it."

Haven saw the four men walking toward him, recognized the one in front as Abe Ellis. He knew Ellis was a man who would hire out for any job. The other three were men he didn't recognize, but he knew the type.

He was not in for an easy time.

* * *

As the four men approached Haven, they spread out in front of him, effectively blocking his way. Even stepping down not the street would not have helped. Other people who were walking by quickly crossed to the other side of the street.

"Hold it, Haven," Abe Ellis said.

"Mr. Ellis," Haven said. "What is this about?"

"Heard you were planning on goin' out of town for a while," Ellis said.

"That's right," Haven said. "Why is that your business, though?"

"I'm makin' it my business," Ellis said. "You stay in town, and me and the boys will buy you some drinks."

"I'm sorry," Haven said, "but I'm not drinkin' now."

"What?" one of the other men said. "The way I hear it, you're always ready for a drink."

Haven squinted at the man and said, "I don't know you. Why do you have something to say about me?"

"Hey," the man said, "I'm just repeatin' what I hear."

"Well, I'll thank you not to comment on what you don't know."

"Listen to this," one of the other men said. "We got us an uppity drunk."

"Stand aside, please, Mr. Ellis," Haven said. "I have business."

"Sorry, Haven," Ellis said, "can't do that. If you don't wanna drink, we're gonna have to break somethin'."

"Break somethin'?"

"An arm, a leg," Ellis said. "Tell you what. We'll let you pick."

"I don't understand," Haven said. "I don't know why

you're doin' this, but I ain't gonna stand still and let you break my arm or my leg."

"You make this hard, Haven," Ellis said, "and it'll come to gunplay. And you're outgunned, four to one."

"Four to two," Clint said, joining Haven on the boardwalk. "Still outgunned, but not as bad."

Ellis stared at Clint, wondering what fool was talking a hand in this, and then realized who it must be.

"Boys, we got us a couple of fools," he said. He figured the other three didn't know they were facing the Gunsmith. Maybe they'd get lucky against him.

He turned and looked at them.

"I think you boys can handle this," Ellis said.

"I think we can," one of them said.

"You boys better wait—" Clint said.

Ellis stepped away and the three men went for their guns before Clint could say anything else, leaving him no choice.

Clint and Haven both drew their guns and fired.

When the shooting started, Ellis slipped away and ran across the street. As he watched the action from there, he saw the Gunsmith draw, and none of the three men ever had a chance. They were dead before they knew it, even before Haven—who had also drawn his gun—could fire.

Ellis turned and ran down the street.

Haven was shocked.

He drew his gun, but before he could fire, Clint Adams had gunned all three men down.

The sounds of the shots faded away and the three men

were on the ground—two were lying on the boardwalk, and one had fallen into the street.

Clint moved in on the bodies, leaned over, and checked to make sure they were all dead. They were, but he kicked their guns away anyway. He then reloaded and holstered his gun.

"Put your gun up, Haven," he said to the tracker. "It's over."

Haven holstered his weapon and said, "What now?"

"We'll just have to wait here."

"For what?" Haven asked.

"The law."

NINETEEN

Sheriff John Cade appeared on the scene very quickly, his gun out. When he saw the three downed men, and Clint, he holstered his gun.

"I guess you better tell me what happened here, Adams," Cade said, "although I can probably guess."

"You've got it wrong, Sheriff—" Clint said, but Haven stepped in.

"He saved my life, Sheriff."

"What?"

"These three—and Abe Ellis—tried to kill me. Mr. Adams stepped in and stopped them."

Cade looked down at the bodies, then looked around.

"I don't see Ellis."

"He ran," Clint said, "when he realized who I was. Only he didn't tell his friends."

"He left them to face you?" Cade asked.

"That's right," Clint said.

"The man was a coward," Haven said.

Cade studied both Clint and Haven for a few moments. Clint figured he was trying to decide whether or not to believe their story.

"Okay, look," Cade said finally, "you'll have to come over to my office with me and make a statement. First I have to get these bodies off the street."

"That's okay, Sheriff," Clint said. "We'll cooperate, but we'd like to make it quick. We have things to do."

"Okay, then, go on over to my office and I'll be right there as soon as I get somebody to move these bodies."

"We'll be there."

As they walked away, the sheriff started looking around for help.

Clint and Haven walked over to the lawman's office and entered.

"Have a seat," Clint suggested to Haven. "We'll get this statement over as soon as he can. Did you know all of those men?" He set his sack of supplies down on the sheriff's desk.

"Just Ellis."

"Ellis?"

"Abe Ellis," Haven said.

"Who does he work for?"

"Whoever pays him."

"Like Kendall?"

"I'm sure he's done work for Kendall," Haven said. "I just don't know if he was working for Kendall today."

"And the others?"

"Just gunhands, I think," Haven said.

"Did Ellis say why he was bracing you today?"

"No," Haven said. "First he said they were gonna hurt me—break an arm or a leg—and then they threatened to shoot me. That's when you stepped in. And by the way, thank you."

"If they were hired guns, they weren't very good," Clint said.

"Good enough to kill me," Haven said. "I'm no hand with a gun, and there were four of them."

"Well," Clint said, "we'll tell the sheriff about Ellis. He might just do his job while we're gone."

"I wouldn't depend on it," Haven said. "He's not very good at his job either."

"Fine," Clint said, "we'll just get this done and get on the trail."

The sheriff came in about ten minutes later, full of apologies.

"Sorry, sorry, it took me a while to find some men to remove the bodies to the undertaker's office."

The man moved around behind his desk and sat. In the next few minutes he took their statements, then sat back in his chair.

"I don't think there'll be any problems with this," he said. "I'll have to check with the judge, of course. But I think he'll agree with me that you had no choice in the matter."

"That's good," Clint said.

"Just don't leave town until I've talked to the judge," Cade said.

"That won't do, Sheriff," Clint said. "We were on our way out of town when this happened. We need to leave, but we'll be back as soon as we've accomplished our goal."

"And what goal is that?"

We need to find two men named Cordell and Underwood."

"I don't know them."

"Well, they worked for Kendall out at his ranch until they were fired."

"And why do you need them?"

Clint decided not to tell the sheriff the whole story.

"We just need to ask them some questions," Clint said. "Haven here is going to track them for me. When we find them, we'll come back."

"I'm afraid you're gonna have to put that off, Mr. Adams," Cade said. "The judge won't like it if you ride out."

"I'll talk to the judge, then," Clint said. "Where is he?"

"In his office, I guess," Cade said, "but I can't go over there with you. I have to see to the men you killed. You'll have to talk to him yourself."

"What's his name?"

"Judge Cade."

"Cade?" Clint asked.

"That's right," Sheriff Cade said. "He's my uncle."

TWENTY

Clint and Haven left the sheriff's office and stopped just outside to talk.

"What do we do?" Haven asked.

"Well," Clint said, "we could just leave town, but that might cause some problems."

"Then what do you suggest?" Haven asked. "You're the boss."

"Why don't you take a ride out to the Kendall ranch and see what you can find out," Clint said, "and I'll go and talk to Judge Cade."

"All right," Haven said. "I can find out where Cordell and Underwood kept their horses and see if there's anything unique about them. After that I should be able to pick up their trail."

"Good," Clint said. "After I've talked to the judge, I'll meet you out there."

"If you don't show up, I'll come back here and find out why," Haven said.

"And you better watch your back," Clint said. "Whoever

sent Ellis and those others after you might try again with some more men."

"I'll be careful."

"See you in a while."

The two men split up from there. Clint walked to City Hall while Haven headed to the livery stable to get his horse.

At City Hall, Clint found that Judge Cade was, indeed, in his office. He was, however, a little busy at the moment consuming an entire chicken. But he agreed to see Clint anyway after Clint introduced himself.

"As long as you don't mind if I continue eatin'," the judge said. "I haven't had much time today."

"I don't mind, Judge."

"Good. Have a seat, then."

The judge was sitting at his desk, and Clint sat across from him. On the desk was a platter with a complete chicken, and another platter of potatoes and vegetables, next to a basket of rolls. The judge's leather chair moaned beneath his 300-plus pounds.

He was pulling the chicken apart with his bare hands, both his sausage-like fingers and his chins—he had more than one—covered and glistening with grease.

"What can I do for you, Mr. Adams?" Judge Cade asked.

"I just came from your nephew's office, Judge—"

"Let me stop you tight there," the judge said, holding up one pudgy hand. "Young Johnny Cade may be my nephew, but he's also the sheriff. And I'm the judge. During business hours that's what we are."

"Okay," Clint said, "I've just come from the sheriff's office. Unfortunately there was an incident on the street where four men tried to kill a friend of mine. I stepped in and I had to kill three of them."

"I heard about that," the judge said, biting into a chicken leg.

"Already?"

"News travels fast in this town."

"Then you know I had no choice."

The judge eyed Clint as he licked his fingers and said, "That *would* seem to be the case."

"Sheriff Cade took statements and asked me not to leave town until he could consult with you."

"That sounds like procedure."

"But I need to leave to track down two men to question," Clint said. "As soon as I find them, I'll be back. He told me I'd have to check with you, though."

"Well," the judge said, "normally I'd need to read those statements."

"Judge," Clint said, "every moment those men are getting further and further away."

"I'm sorry, Mr. Adams," the judge said, "but do you have any official standing with the law that I don't know about?"

"No, sir, I don't," Clint said. "I'm trying to help a friend find out who is targeting him with acts of sabotage."

"Would that friend be Ben Blanchard?"

"Yes, sir."

"So you believe these two men are the ones who tampered with his mine shaft?"

"I do."

"And who are these men?"

"Their names are Cordell and Underwood."

The judge chewed on some breast meat while he mulled over the names.

"I don't believe either of those men has ever been in my court."

"I wouldn't know about that, sir."

The judge put down the piece of chicken he was holding and picked up a white cloth napkin. He began wiping grease from his hands and face, then picked up a small potato and popped it into his mouth.

"I don't see why not," he said then.

"Sir?"

"Hmm? I meant, I don't see why you can't ride out and pursue your . . . prey. Just come back when you're finished."

"Just like that."

"Just like that," the judge said. He picked up a cup of coffee and slurped from it. "I'll clear it with the sheriff." He put the cup down and picked up another big hunk of the chicken. Then he looked at Clint in surprise.

"Are you still here?" he asked. "Go!"

"Yessir."

Ten minutes later Sheriff Cade entered the judge's office. The judge was just finishing his chicken, but he still had potatoes and vegetables to consume. He plucked another potato from the plate and popped it into his mouth.

"Did you see the Gunsmith?" Cade asked.

"I did," the judge said.

"Uncle—"

That drew him a hard look.

"I mean, Judge," Cade said. "What did you tell him?"

"I told him to go," the judge said. "He was interfering with my digestion—as are you."

"Okay, wait," the sheriff said, "you told him he could leave town?"

"Yes."

"But what you meant was . . ."

"That as far as you're concerned," the judge said, "I never told him a thing. Understand?"

"Got it."

"Okay," the judge said. "And where's the other man? Haven? The tracker?"

"I don't know."

"Well, if they actually track down Cordell and Underwood, and they tell Adams they were following Kendall's orders, then we're all in trouble."

"I get it."

"So get yourself a posse, and go out there and get them," Clint said. "Both of them."

"And do what?"

"Do your job, Johnny," the judge said. "Bring them back here and put them in jail."

"Okay, Uncl—I mean, Judge."

"Now get out," the judge said. "I want to finish my meal in peace."

TWENTY-ONE

Clint saddled Eclipse and rode out to the Kendall ranch, looking for Haven. He didn't ride near any of the structures, but circled around the ranch until he spotted the tracker. He was kneeling down, looking at the ground. His horse was behind him, a pinto standing easily while his reins were grounded.

Clint rode up to Haven and dismounted.

"Anything?" Clint asked.

Haven didn't look up, but asked, "How did your talk with the judge go?"

"Too easy," Clint said. "He told me we could leave town, but since he's the sheriff's uncle, I'm not convinced he's not setting us up."

Haven looked up at Clint.

"That bother you?"

Clint thought a moment, then said, "It might, but I'll worry about that later. How about you?"

Haven waved and looked back down at the ground.

"I got an idea after we split up," he said. "I rode out to the salt mine and had a look around. Lots of tracks, but I figured if any of them matched anything here, they might belong to the two men you're interested in."

"That was good thinking," Clint said. "What did you find?"

Haven pointed to the ground, and Clint moved closer to have a look.

"This hoof has a chip in it."

"Enough to make the horse lame?"

"No," Haven said, standing up, "just enough to mark it for us."

"Why don't we make sure?" Clint asked.

Haven nodded. They both mounted up and rode toward the ranch.

Clint decided to go right to the top. They rode up to the house and he walked to the door and knocked. It was answered by Kitty Lane.

"Well," she said, "you're back. Couldn't stay away, huh?"

"We need a favor."

"What can I do for you?" she asked, touching her long hair.

"We'd like to take a look in your barn."

"For what?"

"For wherever Cordell and Underwood stabled their horses."

"And why would you want that?"

"We'd like to see the tracks their horses left."

"Ah," she said, "you're going to track them."

"Yes."

"And is this your tracker?" she asked.

"Yes," he said, "this is Haven."

"Well," she said, "why don't you let Haven have a look in the barn while you come inside and keep me company?"

"Miss Lane—"

"Kitty."

"Kitty, I need to see those tracks as well."

"Those are my terms," she said, folding her arms. "Come inside or get off my property."

Clint looked at Haven, who looked away.

"Okay," he said, "can you have somebody take him over there and show him what stalls their horses were in?"

"Sure. Why don't you go inside and wait in the living room? It's on the right."

"All right." He looked at Haven. "I'll meet you back here."

"I'll be out here," Haven assured him, "waiting."

Clint nodded.

"I'll be right in," she promised Clint.

She took Haven's arm and led him down the stairs, then called out and waved to someone.

Clint went inside.

TWENTY-TWO

Clint was sitting on the sofa when Kitty Lane came back in.

"Your man is being shown to the barn right now," she told him. "Can I get you a drink?"

"No thanks," Clint said. "I don't really have the time."

"It will take your man a while to check those tracks," she said. "One drink? A brandy?"

"Okay," he said. "One drink."

"Good," she said, "very good."

She walked to a sideboard against one wall and poured two brandies from a decanter. She carried them over to Clint, sat next to him, and handed him a glass.

"Here's to life," she said, "and taking advantage of its moments."

"I'll drink to that."

They clinked glasses.

Suddenly, her hand was on his leg. He looked at her, and the expression on her face was wanton.

"Do you know what I mean by life's moments?"

He could feel the warmth of her hand beneath his jeans.

"Kitty—"

She slid her hand up and grabbed his penis through his pants.

"Hmm, I see you do."

"Kitty—" he said again, but now she was rubbing him.

"After you left yesterday, I was wishing I had taken advantage of the situation then. Now I have a second chance." Her hand went to the buttons of her shirt, began to undo them. Before long he saw the swell of her full breasts.

"Kitty, Haven will be back any—"

"He's going to wait outside," she said. "Besides, I told my man to keep him out there as long as he could."

She slipped her shirt off. Had she been expecting him to come back? She was naked beneath her shirt and now her full, brown-tipped breasts were free.

With her other hand she continued to knead his cock through his pants, and he was hardening fast.

"Oh God," she said, squeezing him, "come on, get out of those pants."

She reached for his belt, leaning in and bringing her breasts closer. The scent of her served to inflame him even more, and he reached for her breasts. They were firm in his hands, the nipples hard, the skin warm and smooth.

"Mmmm," she moaned as he thumbed her nipples, and pinched them. He lifted them to his mouth so he could lick them, and then bite them hard.

He finally released them so he could remove his gun belt and set it on the floor within easy reach. Working together, they removed each other's boots and trousers and then he had her on her back. Her pussy was soaking wet and he slid right into her. She gasped, lifted her knees to open herself up even more for him, pressing her heels to his back.

"Oh yes," she groaned as he fucked her, moving in and out of her. She gushed, wetting the sofa beneath her. The smell of her juices filled the air. If someone had entered the room at that moment, she and Clint would not have even noticed.

He strained to fuck her harder, deeper. She gasped. Grabbed at him, exhorted him on as they both took full advantage of this moment.

He gritted his teeth as he came close to exploding, tried to push the urge away, but they were both just too excited. As she gushed again, he exploded into her. She bit her lips in an attempt not to scream, for that would surely have brought some hands running into the house.

Her face turned red, the cords on her neck stood out as she fought back the scream, and he was doing the same, as he wanted to just bellow at the top of his lungs as her insides milked him for all he had . . .

Haven was waiting outside by the horses when Clint and Kitty reappeared. If the tracker suspected anything by looking at them, he didn't let it show in his face.

"Did my man take care of you, Mr. Haven?" Kitty asked.

"It's just Haven, ma'am," he said, "and he seemed a little confused in the beginning, but we got the deed done."

"Did you confirm the tracks are theirs?" Clint asked.

"According to your man, the horse that made those tracks belonged to Cordell."

"All right," Clint said. "I guess we now have something to track."

"I wish you luck," Kitty said as they mounted up. "If those men did what you say they did, I hope you catch them."

"Thanks, Kitty."

"And please," she said, looking directly at Clint, "come back and let me know what happened."

"I'll do that," Clint said. "Don't worry, I'll be back soon."

"Good."

As they rode off, she folded her arms beneath her firm bosom.

Her pussy was still wet.

TWENTY-THREE

They circled around the ranch until Haven was able to pick up the trail again.

"If they were telling us the truth, this is Cordell's trail," Haven said. They had both dismounted and Haven was pointing at the ground.

"How did you read her man?" Clint asked. "Was he truthful?"

"He was stalling me for some reason," Haven said without looking at Clint.

"Whatever it was, at least we now have a trail to follow," Clint said. "When we catch up, we'll find out."

"And I'll know pretty soon," Haven promised, "if they're leading us in circles."

"Good."

They mounted up, and Clint let Haven take a slight lead on him.

"What did the lady have to say?" Haven asked.

"I think she's lonely," Clint said. "She just wanted some company. I had a drink with her."

"Huh," Haven said, "seems to me she's got a lot of men on the ranch who could drink with her."

"Yes, but they work for her," Clint said. "She's the boss."

"I thought Avery Kendall was the boss."

"He is, but she's the foreman . . . I guess."

"I never heard of a woman foreman."

"I haven't either, but apparently she's doing a good enough job for Kendall."

"This way . . ." Haven said, tugging on his horse's reins.

Avery Kendall looked up as Sheriff John Cade entered his office.

"What's on your mind, Sheriff?"

"I'm putting together a posse," Cade said.

"Surely you don't expect me to join."

"No, but I thought you could give me some of your men," Cade said.

"And what's this posse supposed to do?" Kendall asked. "Who are you tracking?"

"Clint Adams."

Kendall sat up straight.

"What?"

"You heard about what happened in the street?"

"Yes," Kendall said. "Ellis came running back to tell me."

"And where is he?"

"I sent him to find Belmont."

"Belmont," Cade said. "I could use him in my posse."

"I have my own work for him to do," Kendall said. "Tell me why you're tracking Adams. Certainly not because of what happened."

"Well, in a way," Cade said. "My uncle—uh, the judge—told Adams it was all right for him to leave town—he's tracking Cordell and Underwood—but he didn't mean it. He says I can now arrest Adams for leaving town during an, uh, active investigation."

"The judge is a shrewd man."

"Yeah, he is."

"Okay," Kendall said, "I'll get you some men, but you can't have Belmont. As I said, I have my own work for him."

"Okay," Cade said. "Have them meet me at my office with their horses and guns."

"Give me an hour," Kendall said.

"Thank you, Mr. Kendall."

"Don't mention it, Sheriff," Kendall said. "Always ready to do what I can to help the law."

Cade left and Kendall sat back in his chair. He doubted the sheriff would be able to take care of Clint Adams, even with a posse to back him up. But if he managed to bring the man back to town, Belmont could get the job done.

He just hoped Cade would find Adams before Adams found Cordell and Underwood.

After Clint Adams left the ranch, Kitty Lane went back into the house and up to her bedroom. She had to change her clothes, which were soaked with her juices, and take a bath because she smelled like sex. Wouldn't do to have her employees smelling that on her.

She immersed herself in a tub and washed herself with soap and a washcloth, lingering between her legs, where she was still very sensitive from Clint Adams's efforts. In fact, she spent so much time touching her pussy that she actually gushed again, her juices mixing with the bathwater.

She hadn't had sex with a man in a long time. It wouldn't be right for her to take one of the hands to her bed, and she'd be damned if she let Kendall touch her. Usually, she satisfied herself in the bath like this, but today she fully remembered what she had been missing—not that she'd ever had a man like the Gunsmith between her legs before. She needed more time with him, time for them to go slowly, time for the man to turn her inside out, which she was sure he could do.

She climbed out of the bath, tried to put Clint Adams from her mind, but even as she dressed in fresh clothes, her pussy quivered, making her shudder.

TWENTY-FOUR

"Well," Haven said, "they're not going in circles."

"That's good," Clint said, "but where *are* they going?"

"There are a few towns in this direction," Haven said. "No point guessing until we get closer."

Clint was surprised at how well, and how sober, the man seemed. He didn't seem to be suffering from being deprived of liquor at all.

"Haven, you mind if I ask you a question?" Clint said.

"Sure, why not?"

"The drinking," Clint said. "What's that about?"

"What do you mean?"

"How can you stay off it while you're working?"

Haven looked at Clint.

"When I'm doin' this," he said, "it's all I care about. When I'm not doing this, there's nothing else I want to do but drink."

"But . . . why is that?"

"I don't know," Haven said.

"Have you ever tried not to drink when you're not tracking?"

"Of course I have," Haven said. "I'm not a stupid man, Clint. It . . . it just doesn't work."

Clint decided to let the man alone. He wasn't a stupid man, and he had his own life to live. There was no reason he had to live his life according to what Clint Adams said.

After all, Clint had his own problems, like an innate inability to stay out of other people's problems.

Ben Blanchard finished walking his mining operation, checking to make sure that everything was progressing the way it should be. His number one shaft was back up and running after having been shut down for a couple of days.

When he reached the foreman's shack—where Mahoney had his office—Mahoney was standing in front, looking over a clipboard. There was a man standing next to him, who looked as if he'd just asked a question and was waiting for an answer. Blanchard finally recognized the man as Joe Lester.

"That's good, Joe," Mahoney said. "Get it done just like that."

"Yessir." Lester took the clipboard and started to walk away, stopped short when he saw Blanchard. "Hello, boss."

"Joe."

Lester moved on. Blanchard joined Mahoney.

"I keep wondering about Adams," Mahoney said.

"Don't worry about Clint," Blanchard said. "He'll get the job done. He'll bring those two men back here if he has to drag them behind his horse."

"Yeah," Mahoney said, "but what if they don't talk?"

"We'll worry about that when they get back," Blanchard said. "First things first—let's get them back to town."

"Yeah."

"I'm going to my office," Blanchard said. "It looks like you have everything under control here."

"Pretty much," Mahoney said.

"What do you think of your watchmen?"

"I had a talk with Davis," Mahoney said. "I actually apologized to him, and then he apologized for falling asleep. I think we're okay."

"And the other man?"

"He's older," Mahoney said, "in his sixties, but he's an ex-lawman and I think he can be trusted."

"That sounds good," Blanchard said. "I guess we're all set until Clint comes back."

"I hope so," Mahoney said. "I'd like to get this business under control before something more serious happens here at the mine."

"Well," Blanchard said, "let's keep our fingers crossed."

TWENTY-FIVE

"Janeway," Haven said.

"What?"

"The town," Haven said. "I think they rode to Janeway."

"What's Janeway like?"

"A mud puddle with a saloon," Haven said. "No law, so it tends to attract men on the run."

"Oh, great."

"It looks like they decided that was the place to hole up," Haven said.

"Is there a telegraph there?"

"No," Haven said. "What are you thinkin'?"

"That maybe they weren't really fired," Clint said. "Maybe they decided to hole up nearby because they're eventually going to be called back to town."

Haven shrugged and said, "We'll just have to bring them back a little earlier than they planned."

"But as far as anybody knows when we ride in," Clint said, "we're on the run ourselves."

"Okay," Haven said. "What about names?"

"We'll figure it out on the way," Clint said.

"I think I'd like to be called 'Bill,'" Haven said.

They rode into Janeway, and Clint immediately saw what Haven meant by calling the town a "mud puddle." The streets were filled with ruts and holes; most of the buildings were at least half fallen down. The ones that still stood were a saloon and a trading post. The town didn't have very much else, except a hotel that looked like a good wind would blow it away.

"What's the population here?" Clint asked.

"Nobody knows," Haven said. "Men come and go so often. But the saloon, hotel, and trading post have one owner."

"So that's three permanent customers?"

"No," Haven said, "one person owns all three."

"And who is that?"

"His name's Elwood Janeway," Haven said. "I think he's in his seventies. He spent a lot of years as an outlaw, came here ten years ago, bought the buildings that were still standing, and renamed the town."

"Janeway," Clint said. "It didn't register to me when you said the name, but I think I remember him. I mean, I never met him, but I've seen his name on posters."

"He was always wanted," Haven said, "and he was never caught."

"If you're going to be an outlaw," Clint said, "that's the way to do it, I guess."

"I guess so."

"Is there a livery stable?"

"Kind of."

"Does Janeway own that?"

"No," Haven said, "it's owned by a man named Tyler Hand. And he owns it because pretty much nobody else ever wanted it."

"I can't wait to see it."

Haven led Clint to the livery, which shocked Clint. It had two walls, held up by two-by-fours pressed into the side of the walls, and braced on the ground. There was a roof, but it was sagging badly on one side. Clint was surprised the two remaining walls were still supporting the roof.

"Jesus," Clint said. "If I put Eclipse in there, the place is liable to fall in on his head."

"Well," Haven said, "we don't have to put up our horses. Let's just find Cordell and Underwood and get out of here."

"I think that's a good idea," Clint said.

"Let's try the saloon," Haven said. "If they are still are, that's where they're likely to be."

They turned their horses and rode back toward the saloon.

They dismounted in front of the saloon, still not having seen one person in town. They had their fake names and stories set, but nobody was asking.

"Wait a second," Clint said before they entered the saloon.

"What?"

"This Elwood Janeway," Clint said. "Does he know you?"

"I don't think so."

"Has he ever seen you?"

Haven hesitated, then said, "Maybe. I was here once before, had a drink in the bar."

"Did you see him?"

"No."

"But he may have seen you."

"He could have," Haven said, "but he wouldn't know my name."

"Haven," Clint said, "you might be taking a chance going in there."

"Well," Haven said, "I'm bein' paid for it, right?"

"Yeah, but—"

"It's my call, Clint," the tracker said. "Come on, let's get this over with."

They went into the saloon.

TWENTY-SIX

Cordell and Underwood had been in Janeway for two days. Every time they went back to their hotel room, they expected the building to fall in on them.

"We gotta get out of this place, Nick," Underwood said to Cordell. "I don't wanna die because a building fell in on me."

"We was told to wait here," Cordell said.

"Well," Underwood said, "I don't even know if I wanna go back to Hutchinson."

"Why not?"

"They got us doin' stuff we wasn't hired to do," Underwood said.

"We're gettin' paid extra for that stuff."

"I know," Underwood said.

"Look, if you don't wanna go back, don't," Cordell said, "but I ain't givin' up this job."

"Okay, okay," Underwood said, "I ain't sayin' I wanna give it up. Not yet anyway."

"Then stop complainin'," Cordell said. "Go get us a coupla more beers."

"Yeah, okay . . ."

As Clint and Haven entered through the batwing doors, Clint said, "If they're here, let me do the talking. In fact, just lay back. This part isn't really your job."

"Don't worry about me," Haven said. "You saved my life already. I can back your play."

"Well, just remember," Clint said. "We need one of them alive."

"Do we know what they look like?" Haven asked.

"I got a description from Ike Davis. It seems that both men are in their thirties, one beefy, one rangy, both tall."

Clint and Haven walked to the bar. There were about a half-dozen men scattered throughout the place, and a bartender behind the bar. Clint didn't see any seventy-year-olds, so he assumed Janeway himself wasn't present.

"You boys in the right place?" the bartender asked.

"We think we are," Clint said. "Two beers."

The bartender eyed them suspiciously, then drew two beers and set the mugs in front of them.

"There's no law here, right?" Clint asked.

"That's right."

"Then we're in the right place."

"On the run?" the man asked.

"Kind of," Clint said. "Actually, we're looking for someone."

"Who?"

"Two men named Cordell and Underwood."

At that moment there was a man at the bar picking up two beers. He picked them up and hurried back to his table. Clint noticed him out of the corner of his eye.

"Never heard of them," the bartender said.

"Yeah," Clint said, "right . . ."

"Look," the bartender said, "there's no shootin' in here. I got a shotgun under the bar—"

"Leave it there," Clint said. "If you make a move for it, I'll have to kill you."

The bartender swallowed.

Clint turned and looked at the two men at the table.

"You look like you saw a ghost," Cordell said to Underwood when he returned with the beers.

"That feller at the bar?" Underwood said. "He just asked the bartender about us."

"Siddown."

"But what if—"

"Siddown, Wes," Cordell said. "Just relax and let me handle it."

Cordell looked at the bar as the man in question turned and looked at them.

"That them?" Haven asked.

"I believe so," Clint said.

"I didn't see any horses outside," Haven said. "They must be in the livery. Should I check—"

"No time," Clint said. "If this is them and we don't move now, we might lose them."

"Well, okay," Haven said. "It's your call."

"Yeah, it is," Clint said, and he set his beer down on the bar. "Come on."

"They're comin' over," Cordell said. "Don't panic, Wes."

"What are we gonna do?"

"Like I said, don't panic," Cordell said. "There's two of them and two of us. The odds are even. Don't move unless I do, understand?"

"I understand."

TWENTY-SEVEN

Clint and Haven approached the table.

"Cordell? Underwood?" Clint asked.

The man who had carried the beers from the bar looked away. The other man stared up at Clint.

"You're mistaken," he said.

"No," Clint said, "you're Cordell and Underwood. You work for Avery Kendall."

"I said you're makin' a mistake," the man said. "I never heard of Cordell or Underwood." He looked at his friend. "Have you?"

"Huh? Oh. N-No," the other man said nervously.

Clint didn't notice the bartender slip from behind the bar and go to a door in the back of the room.

"We followed your trail here, boys," Clint said. "One of your horses has a distinctive marking on his hoof. Why don't we check your horses?"

"I don't think so," Cordell said, pushing his chair back.

"If you go for that gun, I'll kill you," Clint said. He

pointed at Underwood. "If he does go for his gun, I'd stay out of it if I was you. I'll keep you alive. But I only need one of you."

"Don't listen to him, Wes," Cordell said.

"Make up your mind, friend," Clint said.

Neither man moved.

"Which one are you?" Clint asked the other man.

"Um, I'm Underwood."

"Shut up!" Cordell hissed.

"Mister—"

"Adams," Clint said, "Clint Adams."

Underwood's eyes went wide.

"The Gunsmith?"

"That's right."

Underwood pushed his chair back, but he put his hands in the air, far away from his gun.

"I ain't drawin' on you, Adams."

"Just sit tight," Clint said to him. "Let's see if your friend here makes the right decision."

"Wes, you traitor!" Cordell said.

"He's just staying alive, Cordell," Clint said. "Why don't you do the same thing?"

"Let's all just stand fast, boys!" a new voice commanded.

Clint looked without turning his head, saw a man in his seventies standing ramrod tall and straight, wearing a gun like he knew how to use it.

"You'd be Elwood Janeway," Clint said.

"That's right. Did I hear you right?" Janeway asked. "You're Adams?"

"I am."

"It ain't a good idea for you to be in my town," Janeway said.

"I'm not wearing a badge."

"You don't need to be," Janeway said. "You ride around with a target on your back."

"Look," Clint said, "I'm just here for these two men. They have to go back to Hutchinson."

"I thought you said you weren't wearin' a badge."

"I'm not."

"Well, you'll take men out of my town over my dead body," the old man said. "I know who you are, and I'm an old man, but I can still handle a gun. I wouldn't mind tryin' you."

"For these men?"

"For anybody in my town," Janeway said. "Now back off or face me."

"Janeway—" Clint started.

"I tell you what," the older man said. "Let's go into my office and talk. Leave your man out here, and my bartender will keep these two here. Ben?"

"I got 'em, boss."

Clint looked over at the bartender, who had brought his shotgun out from beneath the bar and was pointing it at Cordell and Underwood—or in their direction anyway.

"Whataya say, Adams?"

Clint looked at Janeway and said, "Let's talk."

"This way." Janeway looked at the two seated men. "Either one of you moves, my man will trigger both barrels. Got it?"

"We got it," Cordell said. "But what about him?" he asked, indicating Haven.

"The same goes for him."

"I think I'll just wait at the bar and finish my beer," Haven said.

"Now that sounds like a right good idea, sonny," Janeway said.

Janeway pointed and said to Clint, "It's that door. After you."

"No, that's okay, Mr. Janeway," Clint said, "I'll follow you."

Elwood Janeway grinned, turned, and walked to his office. Clint had to give the man credit for courage, turning his back that way.

TWENTY-EIGHT

Inside the office, Janeway closed the door and said, "Sit down."

The room was small, cramped, with just enough room for a desk, two chairs, and them. Janeway sat behind the desk, groaning as he lowered himself into his chair.

"My old bones don't like this gettin' up and down," he said. "You'll find out when you get to my age."

"I think it's unlikely I'll get to your age," Clint commented.

"I used to feel like that, too," Janeway said. "That's why I retired and came here."

"Really? Retired? Offering to face me for the benefit of those two, I don't call that being much retired."

"Oh, that," Janeway said. "I was kinda hopin' you wouldn't take me up on that."

"Yeah, I'm glad I didn't either," Clint said.

"Why don't you tell me why you want to take those two out of here?"

Clint explained about the sabotage at the mine, and why he suspected the two men.

"So you don't know for sure they did it," Janeway said when he was done. "And they ain't killed anybody."

"No, they haven't."

Janeway shook his head.

"I can't let you take 'em," he said.

"Why not?"

"Word would get around," Janeway said. "I can't afford that."

"Mr. Janeway—"

The old man waved and said, "Don't call me that. Makes me feel even older than I am. Call me Janey."

"Okay, Janey," Clint said. "I need those men. I need what they know."

"And what's that?"

"They know who hired them to sabotage the mine."

"If they did it."

"I'm pretty sure they did."

"I can't let you take 'em on a 'pretty sure.' "

"Well," Clint said, "then we're at an impasse, because I'm taking them."

"Why don't you question them here?" Janeway suggested.

Clint thought about that for a moment. If he took them back with him, he was pretty sure the sheriff wouldn't jail them. In fact, there was no legal reason to take them back. He just needed them to satisfy him with the information he was looking for. He knew Blanchard was thinking the men would testify against Kendall, but the judge was the sheriff's uncle, and Clint was pretty sure they were both owned by Avery Kendall.

"That's an idea," Clint said.

"You can do it right here in the saloon," Janeway said. "But if anybody starts shootin' my place up, I ain't gonna like it."

"Then you better explain that to them."

"I will," Janeway said, "but I'm tellin' you, if you wanna kill 'em, take 'em out into the street."

"I understand."

"Okay then," Janeway said. "Come on, I'll buy you a fresh beer." He groaned as he got up. "Man, it's a sonofabitch gettin' old!"

Back in the saloon, all eyes were on the office door as it opened and Clint and Janeway came out.

"Lower that shotgun, Ben," Janeway said, "and give my friend here a fresh beer."

"Yessir."

"What's goin' on?" Cordell asked. "You lettin' him take us out of here?"

"Nope," Janeway said.

Cordell grinned.

"But I got nothin' against him askin' you some questions here."

"Hey—"

"Just remember," the old man went on, "any gunplay in my place and you'll be sorry. You wanna use your guns, go on outside."

Clint grabbed his fresh beer from the bar and walked over to the two seated men. Underwood was still being careful to keep his hand away from his gun.

"I ain't givin' up my gun," Cordell blustered.

"You don't have to," Clint said. "You go for it and I'll kill you where you sit and deal with the consequences later."

"I ain't touchin' my gun," Underwood promised.

"Good thinking," Clint said. He stared down at Cordell. "How about you?"

"I ain't got a hankerin' to shoot it out with you," he said. "Whataya wanna know?"

"I want to know who put you up to sabotaging the King Street Salt Mine."

"Ah, you're askin' me to sign my death warrant either way," Cordell said.

"Well then," Clint said, "I guess you get to pick how you want to die."

TWENTY-NINE

"I don't wanna die at all!" Cordell said.

"Me neither," Underwood said. "Look, mister, I'm just a ranch hand."

"Then you should have stayed a ranch hand," Clint said, "and not taken on the extra work."

"Adams, if we talk to you, we're dead."

"Seems to me you're out already," Clint said. "You can talk to me right now and just keep on going. Nobody will ever know."

"Y-You don't want us to testify?" Cordell asked.

"Not with the law the way it is in Hutchinson," Clint said. "I don't expect to get much help from the sheriff or the judge. No, you talk to me and I'll take care of the rest myself."

"Tell 'im, Wes," Underwood said. "Tell 'im, or so help me, I will."

"You just wanna know who sent us to the mine?" Cordell asked.

"That's it," Clint said.

"We don't have to give the money back?"

"Keep it," Clint said, "and use it to get as far away from here as you can."

"Well . . . okay," Cordell said. "I'll tell ya."

"Go ahead," Clint said. "Who paid you to sabotage shaft number one at the mine?"

"It was the foreman," Cordell said. "It was Dennis Mahoney."

Clint questioned the men for twenty minutes more, trying to ascertain whether or not they were telling the truth.

"Why would Mahoney hire you?" Clint asked. "He works for Ben Blanchard."

Cordell shrugged.

"I don't know," he said. "All I know is that he did. He paid us to collapse the number one shaft."

"Apparently you didn't do such a good job," Clint said. "They got that shaft back up and running."

"Yeah, he was mad about that," Cordell said. "The watchman saw us, but Mahoney told us he'd take care of that."

And he did, Clint thought. He fired the watchman without bothering to find out what he saw.

Clint looked at Haven, who had been listening the whole time. Janeway had taken a seat while he listened. The bartender was content to stand behind the bar, waiting for orders.

"What do you think?" Clint asked Haven.

"I think he's tellin' the truth," Haven said. "Why wouldn't Mahoney be the guy? Maybe he's lookin' to take over the mine."

"Maybe." Clint turned back at Cordell. "What's Mahoney's connection to Kendall?"

"How would I know?" Cordell asked.

"You work for Kendall."

"We work for Kitty Lane," Cordell said. "She works for Kendall. That man don't even know who we are."

Clint looked at Janeway.

"Sounds right to me," the old man said.

Clint looked at Underwood, who hadn't said a word.

"What do you know?"

"Only what Wes here told me. We were gettin' paid extra money to do a little job."

"That's right," Cordell said. "He only knows what I told him."

"Goddamnit!" Clint swore.

"Can we go now?" Cordell asked.

Clint didn't answer right away. He thought about what he'd learned, and how Ben Blanchard was going to take it. He had brought Mahoney out here from the East to work for him. He trusted him.

"Okay," he said finally, "but if I found out you lied to me, I'll track you down, just like we did this time."

"We got it," Cordell said. "Come on, Wes. Let's get out of here."

The two men stood up. Cordell looked over at Janeway, who gestured for them to go. They went.

"Fresh beers before you go?" Janeway asked Clint.

"I'll take one," Haven said.

"And a whiskey," Clint said.

The three men walked to the bar. The bartender put a beer in front of each of them and gave Clint a shot of whiskey on the side.

"Whiskey's good for bad news," Janeway said. "And I'm assumin' you got some bad news."

"I did," Clint said. He tossed down the shot, chased it

with the beer. "I've got to tell my friend that his foreman is the one trying to shut him down."

"Ouch," Janeway said. "That is bad news."

"Thanks for your cooperation," Clint said.

"Ah, I'm just tryin' to keep the peace here . . . as best I can."

"Like a sheriff," Haven said.

"Ouch," Elwood Janeway said again. "You take that back, amigo."

Clint and Haven left the saloon, mounted up, and left Janeway.

"What are you gonna do?" Haven asked as they rode out of town.

"I'm going to go back and tell Blanchard what I found out," Clint said. "What else can I do?"

"I don't know," Haven said with a shrug. "Keep it to yourself?"

"I could do that," Clint said. "Watch Mahoney, see where he takes me."

"Unless he's doing this for himself," Haven said. "Maybe he *is* tryin' to get the mine for himself."

"That could be," Clint said.

"If you tell Blanchard, he'll fire him right away," Haven said.

"You're right," Clint said. "First I've got to find out if he's working for himself, or for Kendall."

"Or for somebody else."

"Like who?"

Haven shrugged. "Could be somebody else is involved."

"Sure," Clint said, "that's all I need. A new player in the game."

THIRTY

By the time they rode back into Hutchinson, Clint thought he knew how he was going to play it. He was going to tell Blanchard what he had found out, but he wouldn't let him fire Mahoney just yet.

They rode their horses to the livery and dismounted.

"I can take care of the horses if you want to go and see your friend," Haven said.

"Thanks. Come by the mine office later and I'll see you get paid."

"Much obliged."

Clint left the livery and walked to the mining office. He hoped Mahoney wouldn't be there when he walked in. He wasn't. Blanchard was sitting behind his desk, alone in the office.

"I swear," he complained, "I got to hire a girl to handle this paperwork. You back already? One day?"

"Yeah," Clint said, "we found our men at a nearby town."

"Why would they stop nearby?"

"They expected to be called back," Clint said.

"By who?"

"By the man who hired them."

"Kendall?"

"They say no," Clint said.

"And you believed them?"

"I did, Ben."

"So maybe they were working for somebody else who's working for Kendall."

"That's likely."

"So?" Blanchard sat back. "What have you got to tell me, Clint?"

Clint hesitated.

"Bad news?"

"Pretty bad."

Blanchard opened a drawer, took out a bottle of whiskey and two glasses. He filled them both, put one down for Clint, who picked it up. They both drank, then put the glasses down.

"All right," Blanchard said. "It's been all bad news up to now. Let me have it."

"The man who hired Cordell and Underwood to sabotage your mine is . . . Dennis Mahoney."

"No."

"That's what they told me."

"And you believed them?"

"I did, yes."

"Why?"

"They said the watchman, Ike Davis, saw them," Clint said, "but Mahoney told them he'd handle that. And he did. He fired Davis without questioning him first."

"And then you questioned him and found out about the two men. That sonofabitch."

"Right."

"But why?" Blanchard asked. "Why would he do that?"

"Maybe he's looking to take the mine over," Clint said. "Or maybe he's working for somebody."

"Like Kendall?"

"Could be."

"I'll fire his ass!"

"No," Clint said, "don't do that."

"Why not?"

"Because we want to find out if he's acting alone or with somebody."

"So you're going to watch him?"

"That's right."

Blanchard eyed the whiskey bottle, then put it away in the drawer.

"Okay," he said, "I'll play it your way—for now."

"Don't let on to Mahoney, Ben."

"I'll try not to," Blanchard said. "But I'll want to bust his head open."

"Do it later."

"Yeah, okay."

Clint stood up, ready to leave.

"There's something you should know," Blanchard said.

"About what?"

"The sheriff."

"What about him?"

"Soon after he left, he put together a posse and they rode out."

Clint thought he knew the answer but he asked, "Who were they after?"

"From what I heard," Blanchard said, "you."

"Are they still out?"

"Far as I know."

"I wonder where he got the men to ride with the posse," Clint asked.

"From what I heard, they weren't from town."

"Who'd you hear that from?"

"The bartender over at the Dancing Lady."

"I suppose he'd be able to tell me where they came from," Clint said. "Not that I couldn't guess."

"Kendall?"

Clint nodded.

"Well, when he rides back into town, he might try to take you in."

"If he does," Clint said, "he's going to find it easier said than done."

THIRTY-ONE

Before he left, he told Blanchard that Haven would be coming over for his money.

"I couldn't have done the job without him."

"I'll pay him," Blanchard said.

"Pay him well," Clint said.

"Sure."

Clint left the office, figured he'd better go and see the judge before the sheriff came back and tried to arrest him. Because that could get messy.

Very messy.

In another part of town, two men were meeting in an abandoned house, well off the main street. Avery Kendall owned the house and kept it empty, to match the other houses around it.

"You're late," he complained as Dennis Mahoney entered.

"I had work to do," Mahoney said. "I've got to make sure

the mine is running smoothly. After all, it'll soon belong to me."

"Twenty-five percent will belong to you."

"Yes, I know," Mahoney said. "You always remind me."

"But you won't have a tenth of a percent if Adams catches up to those men."

"The sheriff took out a posse. He should have Adams shortly."

"Really," Kendall said. "You have that much confidence in him as a lawman? Even his uncle, the judge, doesn't have that much."

"Well, you gave him the men to get it done with," Mahoney said. "Did you say your man Belmont was with him?"

"That's right."

"I assume you have confidence in him."

"All the confidence in the world," Kendall said, "but after all, we're dealing with the Gunsmith."

Mahoney scoffed.

"We're dealing with an aging legend," he said. "Don't tell me you believe all those stories about him. Dime novel nonsense!"

"You're from the East," Kendall said. "You should have more respect for what has gone before out here in the West."

"Maybe he was a dangerous gunman when the West was truly wild, but civilization has come calling."

"The West is not gone yet," Kendall said.

"It's on its last legs, believe me," Mahoney said.

"I believed you when you said you could get Ben Blanchard to give up the mine," Kendall said. "That hasn't happened yet, has it?"

"I'm still working on it," Mahoney said. "If Adams hadn't

responded to his telegram, it would have been much easier. He really thinks Adams is going to solve his problem."

"Well, you better make sure he doesn't," Kendall said, "or I'm going to forget about our partnership."

"Don't worry," Mahoney said. "I didn't come all this way to fail."

"I hope not," Kendall said. "I'm not used to failure."

Of course not, Mahoney thought. You have the money to buy success whenever you want it.

"Mark my words," Mahoney said. "Next time you see Clint Adams, he'll be riding in with the posse—tied to a horse—if your man Belmont is any good."

"Belmont will make his move when he feels the time is right," Kendall said. "You better be ready to make yours."

"Don't worry about me," Mahoney said. "I've got plans B and C if my plan A doesn't work. That's what makes for success."

"Yes," Kendall said, "*you* tell *me* what makes for success."

Clint went to City Hall, found the judge in his office, this time cutting into a steak at his desk.

"I'm surprised to see you out of jail," the big man said.

"I'll bet," Clint said. "After telling me I was free to leave town, you sent your nephew after me. That wasn't very nice, Judge."

"Well," the man said, picking up a hunk of steak with onions and grease dripping all over it, "I had a change of heart after you left. Changed my mind."

"I see."

"You didn't happen to run into my nephew out there and, uh, kill him, did you?"

"Never saw him," Clint said. "We tracked down the two men we were looking for pretty quick."

"Is that a fact?"

"It is," Clint said. "But if I was you, I'd catch the sheriff as soon as he comes back to town and keep him from trying to arrest me. That will only end badly."

"And I assume you mean for him?"

"Yes."

"Ah. Uh, you wouldn't be interested in his job, would you?" the judge asked. "We could pay you quite well."

"Are you asking me to kill him?"

"No, no, nothing like that," the judge said. "He's my late sister's boy, and I promised her I'd keep an eye on him. No, I'll just take the badge off of him and put it on you. It would be up to you if you wanted to, say, make him a deputy."

"A generous offer, Judge," Clint said, "but I think I'll have to turn it down."

"That's too bad." He took the time to chew another piece of steak before speaking again. A glob of grease fell down onto his vest, taking an onion with it. "Uh, what did you find out when you caught up to those men?"

"Surprisingly," Clint said, "very little. They did say that Avery Kendall didn't have anything to do with hiring them."

"Did they? Did that disappoint you?"

"It did, actually."

"And did they tell you who did hire them?"

"They did," Clint said, "but I'm going to keep that little tidbit of information to myself for now."

"Until . . . what?"

"Until I can get a federal marshal in here."

"A marshal?"

"Yes," Clint said, "I'm afraid I don't have much confidence in the local law around here."

"I assume you include me in that statement?"

"Oh, yes," Clint said. "As far as I'm concerned, you and the sheriff are a package deal."

"I see."

Clint backed toward the door, not sure if the judge had a gun in his desk or not.

"Just tell your nephew to keep away. I'm going to solve this little mystery, and everybody involved will answer to federal law."

"I've had my run-ins with the federal authorities, Mr. Adams," the judge said. "This ain't my first rodeo."

"We'll see, won't we?" Clint asked, leaving the judge's office.

The judge slammed down his knife and fork, upsetting the plate so that grease and onions went flying everywhere. Damn the man for ruining his appetite!

Clint left the building. The judge had seemed very calm—too damn calm—but Clint was hoping he had at least ruined the man's appetite.

THIRTY-TWO

Clint went to the Dancing Lady from City Hall. It was late enough in the day for the saloon to be jumping. He made room for himself at the bar and waved to Mike for a beer. The bartender brought it to him and said, "Glad to see you out and about."

"Why's that?"

"I heard there was a posse out after you," the bartender said.

"Yeah," Clint said, "I just got back from town and heard that, too. But it's being led by Sheriff Cade, right?"

"Right."

"So I guess I don't have that much to worry about," Clint said. "Unless you know something about the men in the posse?"

"Well, they're not a bunch of town clerks, if that's what you think," Mike said. "Cade got some men from Avery Kendall."

"Ah," Clint said, "men who know their way around a gun?"

"Pretty much," Mike said, "but he's also got a man named Belmont riding with him."

"Belmont," Clint repeated. "I don't know that name."

"He's the one Kendall turns to when things get bad," Mike explained.

"We never ran into them out there," Clint said, "so I guess I'll just have to worry about it when they get back."

"If you got to face a whole posse—including Belmont—you're gonna need help."

"Are you offering?"

"Me? No, no, not me," Mike said. "I'm no good if I'm not behind the bar. But you've got Haven, right?"

"I don't know," Clint said. "Do I? He's been paid by now. He's not in here drinking?"

"I haven't seen him."

"Maybe he's at another saloon."

"Haven usually does all his drinkin' here," Mike said. "Maybe he's got another reason for not drinkin' yet."

Clint finished his own drink and set the beer mug down. He was aware that, at some point in time, he had become the center of attention.

"The sheriff made no secret of the fact that he was taking a posse out to find you," Mike told him. "Everybody knows that."

"I see."

"They're all wonderin' what's gonna happen when the posse gets back. I gotta say, I'm wonderin', too."

"I guess we'll all find out when they do get back," Clint said.

It was Belmont who told the sheriff they should go back to town.

"Why?" Cade asked.

"We've lost the trail," Belmont said. "And it wasn't going where I thought anyway. We might have been following the wrong trail from the start."

"So we should go back to the beginning and try to pick it up again," Cade said.

"No," Belmont said, "we should go back to town."

"Why?"

"Adams might be back there already."

They were seated on their horses and riding ahead of the other five men in the posse, so they couldn't be overheard.

"If he's there, I can't arrest him for leaving town during an investigation."

"Sure you can," Belmont said. "You're the sheriff, remember?"

"Yeah, but—"

"And your uncle's the judge," Belmont went on. "He'll back whatever move you make."

"You think so?"

"I do," Belmont said, then he added, "but the truth is, I'll probably have to kill Adams anyway."

THIRTY-THREE

Clint found Haven waiting for him in the lobby of his hotel.

"Did you get paid?" he asked.

"Oh, yeah," Haven said, "Mr. Blanchard was very generous."

"I thought you'd be heading right for the saloon, then."

"Well," Haven said, "I got to thinking."

"About what?"

"The posse."

"Oh, you heard about that?"

"I heard about it around town, and then Mr. Blanchard mentioned it."

"So what's on your mind?"

"I think they'll try to take you when they get back," Haven said. "You're gonna need help."

"You'll stand with me against the posse?"

"I just think that makes more sense than me goin' back to drinkin'."

"Well," Clint said, "I'm not going to try to argue you out of it. But when this is all over, I'll buy you your first drink."

Haven smiled and said, "Deal. So what do we do now?"

"Now," Clint said, "we sit, and wait."

"For what?"

"The posse to get back."

"What about Mahoney?"

"He's going to be real careful about being seen," Clint said, "but I think I know somebody we can depend on to watch him while we wait."

"I knew somethin' was wrong when he fired me," Ike Davis said. "He seemed to blow up for no good reason."

"Well, now we all know the reason."

"So what do you want me to do?" Davis asked. They had found him sitting on a chair in front of his house.

"I want you to watch Mahoney," Clint said. "Follow him without him seeing you."

"And what am I lookin' for?"

"A connection."

"To who? Mr. Kendall?"

"Anyone," Clint said. "I want to find out if Mahoney is working with anyone. Could be Kendall, could be anyone else in town."

"And then what?"

"When you see him with someone, you let me know."

"That's it?"

"That's it."

"And what about my job as night watchman?"

"Keep doing that," Clint said. "I don't want to take a chance on Mahoney knowing that we know what he's up to."

"Well, okay," Davis said. "Am I gonna get paid for this?"

THIRTY-FOUR

The posse rode back in the next day.

Ike Davis went to work that night, stood watch at the mine, and then in the morning started following Dennis Mahoney.

Clint was getting dressed in his room when he heard the horses on the street. He looked out the window, saw the posse come riding in and stop in front of the sheriff's office.

When he came down to the lobby, Haven was waiting there for him.

"They're in," the tracker said. "They probably camped last night and started ridin' back at first light."

"Have you had breakfast?" Clint asked.

"No, but—"

"Come on," Clint said. "I'm buying."

When the posse reined in their horses in front of the sheriff's office, Cade and Belmont dismounted.

"Take care of the horses, and stay in town," Belmont told the other men. "We ain't done yet."

"Okay," one of them said.

As Cade and Belmont went inside, the rest of the posse rode for the livery stable, taking their horses with them.

Inside Cade said, "So now we go looking for Adams."

"Not yet," Belmont said.

"Why not?"

"Because by now he's heard that you formed a posse to track him down," Belmont said. "He knows about it. He'll be expecting you."

"Yeah, you're right."

"Relax, Cade," Belmont said. "Let's get some breakfast. I don't think Clint Adams is gonna be hidin' anywhere, do you?"

"Probably not. But what if he found Cordell and Underwood?" Cade asked.

"It don't matter," Belmont said. "I'm gonna take care of Adams once and for all."

"When?"

"In my own time," Belmont said. "First, I want a hot breakfast."

"Shouldn't we let Mr. Kendall know we're back?"

"Believe me, Cade," Belmont said, "everybody knows we're back."

Belmont was a tall, thin man, not imposing looking at all, but because Cade knew how good Belmont was with a gun, he was afraid of him. So if Sid Belmont wanted breakfast, that was what they were going to get.

Over breakfast Clint said to Haven, "Tell me what you know about this Belmont."

"Sid Belmont," Haven said. "He's the deadliest gun in these parts."

"Fast?"

"Real fast."

"How old is he?"

"I don't know," Haven said. "My age, I guess. Thirties."

"Does he work for Kendall?"

"He has worked for Kendall," Haven said. "He works for whoever's got the money."

"Well," Clint said, "in this town that sounds like Kendall."

"There's somebody else he's worked for . . . a lot," Haven added.

"Oh? Who's that?"

"The judge."

"Judge Cade?"

"He's the only judge in town."

"No circuit judges come here?"

"Cade won't allow it. And he's got a lot of power . . . politically, I mean."

"So what will happen if I try to bring a federal marshal in here?"

"The judge will send a telegram," Haven said, "and probably get his way. So you better have some connections of your own if you're going to do that."

"I have some federal connections," Clint said. "I guess I better send out a telegram before I do anything else."

"Sounds like a good idea to me."

Judge Haven looked down at the town from his window. When the door to his office opened, he turned.

"You sent for me, Judge?" Abe Ellis asked.

"That's right," the judge said. "I heard the posse ride back into town."

"Yessir."

"Has Kendall talked to Belmont yet?"

"Not that I know of, sir."

"And I haven't heard from my nephew," Judge Cade said. "So I want you to find him and tell him to get his ass up here."

"Yessir."

At that moment a waiter from a nearby café appeared at the door with the judge's breakfast.

"That's all, Ellis."

"Yessir."

"William," the fat man said, "good to see you. Just put everything right on my desk."

THIRTY-FIVE

Clint and Haven finished their breakfast, left the hotel, and Haven showed Clint the way to the telegraph office.

Inside Clint wrote two telegrams and handed them to the clerk.

"Uh, you're Clint Adams?" the clerk asked.

"That's right."

"Um," the young man said, his Adam's apple bobbing, "I'll have to send these a little later. I'm kinda busy."

"That's okay," Clint said. "I'll come back later for the replies."

"O-Okay."

Clint and Haven left.

After they were gone, the clerk hurriedly removed his apron and visor, put on his hat, and practically ran to the door. He stopped outside to lock it behind him, but when he turned, he ran straight into Clint Adams and bounced off.

"Where are you going, son, with my telegrams?"

They had the clerk unlock the door and they all went back inside, where Clint asked him again.

"Um, well . . ."

"Suppose I guess," Clint said. "You were going to show them to Judge Cade, who told you to be on the lookout for me, in case I wanted to send some telegrams."

"Uh, yeah."

"And you do everything the judge tells you to do?"

"Well . . . everybody in town does."

"Okay," Clint said, "so when the judge asks you why you sent those telegrams without telling him, you can tell him I held my gun on you."

"B-But he'll—he'll—"

Clint drew his gun and pointed it at the clerk. He never drew his gun unless he was going to fire it, but he did this for effect.

"Send them."

"Yessir."

The clerk got behind the desk, sat at the telegraph key, and sent both telegrams.

"There," the clerk said. "Can I go now?"

"Go where? Don't you have to work?"

"I—I'm too nervous to work."

"It's all over now, kid," Haven said.

"Actually," Clint said, "it's not."

"Why not?"

"Because we're going to wait right here for the replies," Clint said.

"We are?" Haven asked.

"We are?" the clerk asked.

"We are," Clint said.

* * *

It took twenty minutes for both replies to come in.

"Okay," Clint said to the clerk when he handed him the second one, "now you can go."

"Go? Go where? When the judge finds out—"

"What's your name, son?"

"Eddie."

"Well, Eddie," Clint said, "why does the judge have to find out anything?"

"Whataya mean?"

"I mean if you tell the judge you sent these telegrams, you're in trouble, right?"

"Right."

"Then don't tell him."

"B-But if he finds out—"

"How's he going to find out?" Clint asked. "If you don't tell him, we won't tell him."

Eddie stared at them for a moment, then said, "Wait . . . really?"

"Really," Clint said. "Besides, you read those telegrams, right?"

"Well, I had ta, in order to send 'em—but I don't have ta remember what they said!" Eddie told them. "I mean, if you don't want me—"

"Don't worry about that," Clint said, cutting him off. "Relax. It just matters that you read them. You know that the judge is going to be in a lot of trouble when the federal marshal gets here, and will probably lose his seat on the bench."

Eddie looked from Clint to Haven and back again.

"Wait . . . really?"

"Really."

"He won't be the judge in Hutchinson anymore?" Eddie asked them.

Haven shook his head.

"He won't be the judge anywhere anymore," Clint said. "Or ever again."

Eddie smiled and said, "That's good."

Clint smiled back and said, "That's very good."

THIRTY-SIX

"You want to tell me who you sent telegrams to?" Haven asked as they walked away from the telegraph office.

"Judge Parker, for one."

"Hanging Judge Parker? That Parker?"

"That's right."

"He's in Missouri."

"Arkansas," Clint said, "but that doesn't matter. He's a federal judge. He can get things done."

"So he's gonna get a marshal sent here?"

"Yes."

"Who else?"

"Friend of mine named Talbot Roper," Clint said. "He's a private detective in Denver."

"Why him?"

"I just wanted somebody to know what was going on here," Clint said. "If he doesn't hear from me again in a few days, he'll send somebody in."

"You expectin' to die?" Haven asked.

"I'm always expecting to die," Clint said.

"Why?"

"That way I'm never disappointed."

Ellis found Sheriff Cade sitting with Sid Belmont in a café.

"Sheriff," he said, "the judge wants you right now."

Cade looked down at his half-eaten meal.

"Relax, Abe," Belmont said. "Have a seat, some coffee. Maybe somethin' to eat."

"But the judge is waitin'."

"Let him wait," Belmont said. "The sheriff hasn't finished his breakfast."

Ellis stared at the two men helplessly, then pulled out a chair and sat. It was actually past breakfast time, so the café was otherwise empty. The waiter came over and Ellis ordered ham and eggs.

"The judge is gonna kill me," he said.

"Don't worry," Belmont said, "the sheriff will handle the judge."

"I will?"

"Well, sure. He's your uncle, right?"

"First he's the judge," Cade said. "That's the way it's always been."

"So he's not much of a family man?" Belmont asked.

"I don't know," Cade said. "He told my mother he'd look after me, and he has."

"By makin' you sheriff," Belmont said.

Cade nodded.

"Does he respect you?"

"Oh, no," Cade said. "Not at all."

"Doesn't that bother you?" Ellis asked.

Cade shrugged.

"The judge is the judge."

"Aren't you afraid of him?" Ellis asked.

Cade thought a moment, then said, "When I was a kid, I was, but not now."

"Why not?" Belmont asked.

"Well . . . he is my uncle, after all."

"But," Ellis said, "he scares everybody else in this town."

"Almost everybody," Belmont said.

"Well, yeah . . ." Ellis said.

"I'll go back to the judge's with the two of you," Belmont said. "I'll tell him what we're plannin'."

"I think I should tell him, Sid," Cade said. "After all, I'm the sheriff."

"Okay, Sheriff," Belmont agreed. "You tell 'im—I mean, since you ain't scared of 'im."

THIRTY-SEVEN

"How are we gonna play this?" Haven asked as they entered the Dancing Lady Saloon.

"We're not going to go looking for trouble," Clint said, "but we're not going to hide either."

"So the saloon is neutral ground?" Haven asked.

"We'll see."

Clint motioned to Mike for two beers. He looked around. The place was more empty than full. The girls weren't working yet, the gaming tables were covered, and nobody was looking at him. Maybe they had lost interest, or maybe nobody wanted to look at him because they figured he was wanted—or as good as dead.

"The word's out," Mike said, setting down the two beers. "You're both wanted."

"Both?" Haven asked.

"Mostly Clint," Mike said, "but you were with him when the shooting happened."

"He was with me," Haven said. "Saved my goddamned bacon."

"Well, there ya go," Mike said.

"Do you think they'll come in here for us, Mike?" Clint asked.

"Probably not," Mike said. "They'll wait for you to step outside."

"Suits me, then," Clint said. "If you don't mind, we'll just have a few beers to get ready."

"Suit yourself," Mike said. "Just wave at me when you want more."

Ellis entered the judge's office and said, "Uh, Judge, the sheriff and Belmont are here."

"Send them in!"

"Uh, and me?"

"Go away!"

"Yessir."

Ellis withdrew. Moments later Cade and Belmont appeared and entered the room. Cade saw plates on the desk, but they had been plowed through. He couldn't remember the last time he saw his uncle at his desk *not* eating.

"Judge," Belmont said.

"Sir," Sheriff Cade said.

"Don't tell me, let me guess," the judge said. "You didn't catch Clint Adams."

"Uh, no, sir," the sheriff said.

"You want to know how I know?" the judge asked.

"No, sir," Cade said, "I mean, yes, sir."

"He came to see me yesterday," the judge said, "Told me to tell you not to try to arrest him."

"He told you that?"

"He did!"

"But . . . I have to try."

"Yes, you do." The judge looked at Belmont. "And you'll back his play."

"Hey, I rode with his posse," Belmont said, "but I ain't a deputy. I don't have a badge, and don't want one."

"I don't care whether you have a badge or not," the judge said. "What I want is your gun."

"My gun don't come cheap, Judge."

"I know that, damn it!" Judge Cade said. He touched his stomach, leaned back in his chair, which groaned. "Okay, now you're affecting my digestion."

"Sorry, Uncl—I mean, Judge."

"Son," the judge said, "you better get this done and get it done quick."

"Yessir."

"Now get out, the both of you. Go find the rest of your posse."

Sheriff Cade nodded and led the way out of the office.

Cade and Belmont found Ellis waiting outside.

"Okay," Belmont said to him, "get the rest of the posse together, tell them to meet us at the sheriff's office."

"Should I tell them why?"

"To do what they're bein' paid to do."

"A dollar a day?" Ellis asked.

"Just do it!"

"Yeah, okay, Sid."

"What about us?" Cade asked.

"We'll go back to your office and wait," Belmont said. "Once we have all the men together, we'll go and 'arrest' Clint Adams."

"Suits me," Cade said.

* * *

While Haven and Clint were working on their second beers, Haven asked, “Shouldn’t we maybe take a more aggressive role in this?”

“How so?” Clint asked. “Go out and find the posse ourselves?”

“No, not the whole posse,” Haven said. “Maybe just the sheriff.”

“And do what?”

“Question him,” Haven said. “Get him to admit that the judge set us up to be arrested by telling you that it was all right for us to leave town.”

“I’m not after the judge, though,” Clint said. “It’s Kendall we want.”

“I thought it was whoever Mahoney was working for,” Haven said. “And that might not be Avery Kendall.”

“You’re right,” Clint said. “He could be working for the judge.”

“Or for himself.”

“Mmm, I don’t think so.”

“Why not?”

“The sheriff got his posse men from Kendall,” Clint said. “Why would that be if Kendall wasn’t involved? Why would he care if we got caught or not?”

Haven stared into his beer mug.

“I don’t have an answer to that one,” he said, “but I have another suggestion.”

“What’s that?”

“Maybe they’re all in it together.”

“Well, if that’s the case,” Clint said, “maybe we can take them all down at the same time.”

THIRTY-EIGHT

"All right," Belmont said, "now that we're all here, let's get down to business."

"I thought the sheriff was in charge," one of the posse men said.

"He is," Belmont said. "He's just lettin' me do the talkin'."

"So talk."

"The Gunsmith is in town," Belmont said.

"Is he alone?" one of the man asked.

"No," Belmont said, "but he's only got one man backin' his play."

"So you think we got enough men to handle them both?"

"I'll handle the Gunsmith," Belmont said. "The rest of you can take care of Haven."

"Haven?" a man named Vince Powers asked.

"You know him?" Belmont said.

"A few of us know him," Powers said, and a couple of men nodded.

"Well, I know 'im, too," Belmont said. "That doesn't matter. He picked his side."

"So when do we do this?" one of the other men asked.

"Right now," Belmont said. "We take to the street and find them both."

"Haven will probably be in a saloon," Powers said.

"Right," Belmont agreed. "Probably the Dancing Lady."

"Then let's go," Sheriff Cade said.

A man came into the saloon, approached the bar, and spoke urgently to Mike the bartender.

"Something's happening," Clint said to Haven.

Mike came over to where Clint and Haven were standing.

"You fellas better go on out the back," he said.

"Why?" Clint asked.

"The posse is on its way."

"How many?" Haven asked.

"Seven," Mike said.

"Are the sheriff and Belmont with them?" Clint asked.

"Yes," Mike said, "right in the front."

Clint and Haven exchanged a look.

"Well," Clint said, "this is what we've been waiting for, isn't it?"

"Maybe it's what you've been waitin' for," Haven said.

"Back door's there," Mike said, "in case you change your mind."

"Thanks, Mike," Clint said.

They set their beers down on the bar and walked over to the batwing doors. From there they watched the street.

Ellis found Mahoney, managed to get him alone, just outside the mining office.

"What?" Mahoney said. "You know you're not supposed to be seen with me."

"I know, but Belmont sent me over."

"Since when is Belmont in charge?"

"Well, you tell 'im he ain't," Ellis said. "Meanwhile, the posse is on its way to kill the Gunsmith."

"Good," Mahoney said. "It's about time we got rid of him. Without him around, we can get back to work."

"Do you wanna go watch?"

"No," Mahoney said. "Are you crazy? I don't want to be anywhere near there when it happens."

"Okay," Ellis said, "but I wanna watch."

"That's what you should do, Ellis," Mahoney said. "Watch and let me know when it's over—but don't come here!"

"Yeah, okay," Ellis said, "but when it's all over, the whole town will probably know what happened."

"That's fine," Mahoney said. "Now . . . go!"

After Ellis left, Mahoney wondered what he should do next. Where should he be when Clint Adams was killed? Probably with Ben Blanchard. What would be a better alibi than that?

He turned and went into the mining office.

As Mahoney entered, Blanchard looked up at him. It was all he could do not to take the gun from his desk and shoot him.

"What's going on?" Blanchard asked.

Mahoney sat across from Blanchard.

"I'm just looking for a place to do some thinking," Mahoney said.

"About what?"

"About everything, Ben," Mahoney said. "About everything."

Blanchard took out the bottle and the two glasses. The gun was right next to the bottle. He left it there.

"You want a drink while you're thinking?" he asked.

Mahoney leaned forward, reached for a glass, and said, "I thought you'd never ask."

THIRTY-NINE

"Here they come," Haven said.

"Seven, like Mike said."

"I can count."

"If I take care of Belmont and the sheriff, the others might give up."

"And what do I do?" Haven asked.

Clint looked at him and said, "The best you can."

"That's Belmont in front," Haven said. "The tall one." He looked at Clint. "Remember, he's good. Don't hold back."

"I won't."

As the posse came closer, Haven asked, "What's the most men you've ever killed at one time? In a gunfight? And I mean in one draw, not a running gun battle."

"Five."

"Five?" Haven said, obviously impressed. "Really? How many times have you done that?"

"A few," Clint said, "but there was no Belmont involved. I mean, if he's as good as you say he is."

"He is."

"Okay, then," Clint said. "I'll just have you make sure I take him first."

"Forget about the sheriff," Haven said. "We can leave him for last. He's not very good."

"Gotcha," Clint said.

"How good is Haven?" the sheriff asked Belmont.

"I don't know," the gunman said. "He's a helluva tracker the way I hear it, but I never heard anything about how he is with a gun. But don't worry about him. "We'll have to take the Gunsmith first."

"If he's even in the saloon," Powers said.

"If he's not, we'll just find him someplace else," Belmont said.

"I don't think that's gonna be necessary," Sheriff Cade said.

"What—" Belmont stated, but he stopped when he saw the two men who had stepped out the batwing doors of the Dancing Lady.

"That's him," Cade said.

"Good," Belmont said. "Then we can get this done right now."

"Why are they just standin' there?" Powers asked.

"What else are they gonna do?" Belmont asked.

"Run?" Powers asked.

"Not the Gunsmith," Belmont said. "He didn't get his reputation by runnin'."

"I suppose not," Cade said.

Belmont stopped walking, turned to face the members of the "posse."

"I'll kill the first man who breaks and runs, understand?" he said.

They all nodded.

"All right," Belmont said, "let's take 'em."

"Do we just wait here?" Haven asked.

"Yes," Clint said. "Don't step into the street unless I do."

"Got it."

"And don't worry about Belmont," Clint said. "He's mine. Just concern yourself with the others."

"The other six?"

"I don't expect you to handle them all," Clint assured him.

"Well, that's good."

"Just stand about an arm's length from me," Clint said. "And be ready for anything."

"You know," Haven said, "right about now I could use a drink. I mean a real drink."

"After," Clint said.

FORTY

The posse reached the saloon and stopped. Belmont stepped forward. Sheriff Cade was to his right, one step back. The rest of the posse fanned out behind them, which suited Clint. Spread out, they were all targets. Clustered, some would have shielded the others.

"Clint Adams," Sheriff Cade said, "you're under arrest. You, too, Haven. Put down your guns and come with us."

"I'm not giving up my gun, Sheriff," Clint said. "That kind of thing tends to get people like me killed."

"If you don't comply, then you're resisting arrest."

"Okay then," Clint said, "I'm resisting arrest. Now what?"

"We'll have to take you by force," Belmont said.

Clint looked at the tall man.

"You must be Belmont."

"That's right."

"I don't see any deputy badges," Clint said.

"We're not deputies," Belmont said, "but we're backin' the sheriff's play."

"Well, that's good."

"Why is it good?"

"It's good to know I'll only be killing one lawman today, and not seven."

"Big talk for a man who's facing worse than three-to-one odds."

"I figure I'm even money," Clint said.

Belmont smirked.

"How do you figure that?"

"My main concern is you," Clint said. "So I'm going to kill you first. Once you're dead, I figure the odds even swing in my favor."

Belmont shook his head.

"Big talk for a man depending on his reputation."

"Reputation's got nothing to do with it," Clint said. "For instance, they tell me you're pretty good with a gun. I can't count on that, though. I've got to see for myself."

"Oh, you will," Belmont said.

"Why do I get the feeling you're the one calling this play, not the sheriff?"

"Like I said," Belmont replied, "were backin' the sheriff's play."

"I'm actin' on authority of the judge, Adams," Cade said.

"Then I guess your uncle will be real upset when he hears you died trying," Clint said. "Or maybe he'll be proud. Who knows?"

"Enough talk," Belmont said.

"I agree," Clint said. "Go for your gun, Belmont. You're going to be first."

Judge Cade could see the action in front of the Dancing Lady from his office window. He was standing while he watched, wondering what all the talking was about. It took so long that his legs couldn't hold his considerable weight, so he pulled his chair over to the window and sat.

Get it done already!

The first move was left to Belmont, and he took it.

As he went for his gun, Clint could see that the man had earned his reputation. He was fast. He didn't know how deadly he'd be with the gun in his hand, and he wouldn't find out, because he didn't give the man a chance. As fast as Belmont was, Clint outdrew him cleanly and shot him before he cleared leather.

From his window Judge Cade saw Belmont go down without getting his gun out.

"Sonofabitch!" he swore.

Haven drew and fired. He was not fast, but he was accurate. He dropped to one knee and fired coolly. Two men spun then fell in the street.

Haven didn't see what Clint was doing, but he heard the Gunsmith's gun fire incredibly quickly, as if the man was fanning the hammer—which, of course, was what Clint was doing.

Most men could not fire accurately when they fanned the hammer. They didn't allow for the jerky motion, which would normally lift the barrel and spoil the aim. Clint, however, had long ago mastered the art, and the barrel of his gun was steady as he fired.

Haven's hammer fell on empty chambers and he wondered if he was going to have time to reload—or if he would even have to.

Suddenly, it was quiet. The only sound to be heard was the groaning of injured men.

"You all right?" Clint asked. "Are you hit?"

"No," Haven said, "I don't think so."

He watched as Clint quickly ejected his spent shells and reloaded. Haven had never seen anyone do that so fast.

FORTY-ONE

Clint walked among the fallen men, found five dead and two wounded. One of the wounded was Sheriff Cade.

There were a bunch of men on the boardwalk in front of the saloon.

"Somebody go and get the doctor!" Clint shouted. "And find some deputies."

Two men separated themselves from the crowd. Across the street more people congregated, men and women.

"He shot the sheriff," Clint heard somebody say.

"Somebody should do somethin'," another voice added.

Clint stood straight and said to the crowd, "If anybody wants to do something you better step up and do it now. Otherwise break it up and move on. There's nothing more to see here."

Slowly, the crowd began to disperse.

From his window the judge continued to watch. All seven men looked dead to him, until he saw two of them move.

He could not tell, from where he was, if one of them was his nephew, the sheriff.

He turned as the door to his office opened and Ellis came rushing in.

"Judge—"

"I saw."

"What do we do now?"

"Is the sheriff dead?"

"I don't think so."

"Belmont?"

"First one."

The judge thought a moment, then said, "You better go and tell Mr. Kendall that we have to meet."

"Yessir!"

Ellis ran out, closing the door behind him. As the judge directed his attention out the window again, he saw the doctor walking quickly toward the fallen men . . .

As a middle-aged man in shirtsleeves approached, Clint asked, "Are you the doctor?"

"No," the man said, "I just carry an extra shirt in this black bag!"

"Five of these men are dead," Clint told him.

"You mind if I be the judge of that?" the doctor asked.

"You better check on the sheriff first, though."

"Shit," the doctor said. He looked at the seven men, picked out the lawman, and knelt next to him. "Lie still, Cade."

"Am I gonna die?" Cade asked.

"Yes, if you don't lie still and let me examine you." Clint wasn't sure about the doctor's bedside manner, but he liked the man and thought he was probably a pretty good physician.

Clint stood and watched while the doctor examined the lawman.

"It's the shoulder," he said, tearing the shirt so he could get a better look. "Looks like the bullet went all the way through. Don't know if it hit anything crucial."

Clint wasn't sure if the doctor was talking to him or the lawman—probably him.

The doctor put a temporary bandage on it, then stood up and faced what was left of the crowd.

"I need two men to carry the sheriff to my office. Now!"

Two men rushed into the street to do as they were told.

The doctor looked at the other six men, found that Clint was right. There was only one other man alive.

"Vince Powers, right?" the doctor asked.

"Right, Doc," Powers said. "Is it bad?"

"Be still and let me look."

It was a hip injury. The doctor packed it and got two more men to carry Powers to his office.

"Somebody will have to see that these men are carried to the undertaker," he said to Clint.

"Not my job, Doc," Clint said. "A deputy should see to that."

"The deputies are as much idiots as the sheriff is," the doctor said. "You shoot these men?"

"I did," Clint said.

"So did I," Haven said.

The doctor looked at him and said, "I know you, don't I? Treated you before?"

"A time or two."

"Haven, right?" the man asked,

"That's right."

"You still owe me two dollars."

Haven didn't answer.

"Look, I don't care whose job it is," the doctor said, "I want these men cleared off the street and taken to the undertaker's."

Haven looked at Clint, who looked away, so the tracker said, "Sure, Doc."

The doctor gave Clint a hard look and said, "I hope there was a good reason for all this carnage." He didn't wait for an answer, just stormed off.

Haven looked around at the dead bodies.

"Was there?" he asked.

"I guess we're going to find out."

Clint looked at what was left of the crowd, saw Ike Davis standing there. He walked over to him.

"Where's Mahoney?"

"In the mining office with Blanchard."

"What are they doing?"

"Last I saw, they was just sittin', havin' a drink."

"Figures," Clint said. "He's setting up an alibi for himself."

Haven came over to stand with them.

"You ever see Mahoney go near Kendall or the judge?"

"Nope," Davis said.

Haven looked over to where some men were now picking up the bodies.

"The sheriff comin' after you, that would mean the judge is involved," he said. "Belmont coming after you, that could mean it's Kendall, too."

"So Kendall and the judge are working together," Clint said. "Ben brought in Mahoney, and they bought him. Is that the way you see it?"

"I think that's your worst-case scenario," Haven said.

"Belmont does most of his work for Kendall these days," Davis said, "so that would be the way I see it, too."

"All right," Clint said, "the last move was theirs, the next one has to be ours."

"And what would that be?" Haven asked.

"I'm thinking," Clint said, "I'm thinking . . ."

FORTY-TWO

"We split up," Clint said finally.

"We?" Davis asked.

"I mean me and Haven," Clint said. "You're done, Ike."

"I still got my night watchman job?"

"You do."

"So where are you fellas goin'?"

"I'm going to go and see the judge," Clint said.

"Guess that leaves Kendall for me," Haven said.

"Do you know him?"

"Some."

"Well, he'll know that you and I are working together," Clint said.

"That's okay," Haven said. "I've never liked men with money anyway."

"I can do somethin'," Ike said.

"Yeah, you can," Clint said. "Go and tell Blanchard what happened here. Tell him to stay put."

"And if Mahoney is there?"

"Just act like you don't suspect a thing."

"Okay," Davis said, "but what are you fellas gonna do to the judge and Kendall?"

Clint shrugged and said, "Whatever comes natural, I guess."

Clint thought there was very little chance the judge would not be in his office when he got there. The fat man obviously did not move around very easily. Sure enough, Judge Cade was seated behind his desk, but with no food in front of him. On a more slender man Clint might have said his face was drawn.

"I suppose you had a front row seat from your window," Clint said. "Did you like what you saw?"

"I did not," the judge said.

"Of course not," Clint said. "You were expecting—hoping—to see me shot down in the street."

"That's ridiculous."

"Is it? You sent your nephew and Belmont after me."

"Belmont works for Avery Kendall," the judge said.

"And how do I know you don't?" Clint asked.

The judge made a rude noise with his mouth and said, "That's preposterous, sir."

"So then, he works for you?"

"Much more likely," the fat man said, his hands clasped over his belly, "but no."

"So I get one more guess," Clint said. "You're working together to take control of Ben Blanchard's mine. And to do that, you bought his foreman, Mahoney."

"You can't prove—"

"This isn't a court of law, fat man!" Clint snapped. "I

don't have to prove it to you. I only have to prove it to me, and I have."

"You can't appoint yourself judge and jury."

"Not only can I appoint myself judge and jury," Clint said, "but executioner as well."

For the first time since he'd met the man, the judge looked uncomfortable—possibly even nervous.

"You wouldn't dare," the fat man said.

"Why not?" Clint asked. "I've already shot a sheriff. Why not a judge, too?"

"Now hold on—"

"You know my reputation," Clint said. "I'm a killer, right?"

"I'm—I'm—" the judge stammered, holding both chubby hands out in front of him, as if to shield himself from a hail of bullets. "You can't—"

"There's only one way I don't kill you here and now," Clint said.

"H-How—what—why?"

"Give me Kendall," Clint said. "And back off of Blanchard's mine. Was it your idea, or Kendall's, to go after it?"

"It was his," the judge said, "all his. He came to me with the idea."

"And offered you what?"

"H-He was going to give me enough to launch a campaign," Cade said.

"Oh, yes, politics," Clint said. "I'm afraid that future isn't very bright for you, Judge."

"What?"

"No, that's another condition of not killing you," Clint said. "This office is as far as your authority will ever go."

"You can't mean—"

"I do," Clint said. "Oh, I do. The federal marshal will be here, probably tomorrow. What I tell him then depends on what you do today."

"You mean . . . you might not—"

"I might not say the wrong thing where you're concerned," Clint said. "I'm only concerned with Ben Blanchard keeping his salt mine and not having to worry about further sabotage."

Judge Cade cleared his voice, striving to sound more in charge of the situation.

"I think you can depend on that, Mr. Adams," he said.

"You'll talk to Avery Kendall?"

"Kendall will do what I tell him," Cade said, "never fear."

"Well, that's good," Clint said. "It also better be true."

"Don't worry," Judge Cade said. "You don't have to worry about your friend anymore."

"We'll see," Clint said. He started for the door, then turned and said, "By the way, your nephew's going to be fine. I knew you'd be worried."

Blanchard and Mahoney listened to the news as Ike Davis delivered it.

"So Clint Adams isn't dead?" Mahoney asked.

"No sir," Davis said. "He shot those men down slicker 'n snot."

"The sheriff, too?" Blanchard asked.

"Him, too, only he ain't dead."

Blanchard looked at Mahoney, who was frowning.

"Bad news for you, huh, Dennis?"

"Hmm? What?"

"You were hoping Clint would be dead and you could go on with your sabotage."

"Ben, I—"

"You're fired, is what you are," Blanchard said. "Go and tell your boss—Kendall, Judge Cade, or whoever it is—that you're out of a job."

Mahoney stood up and glared at Blanchard.

"You can't do this!"

Blanchard opened his drawer and took out his gun.

"Get out before I decide that firing your ass isn't good enough!"

Mahoney stared at Blanchard a few moments, then obviously decided that the man would shoot him. He moved toward the door. As he passed Ike Davis, the night watchman said, "If I was you, I'd leave town. Clint Adams has got a federal marshal comin' to town tomorrow. I heard the government don't take well to sabotage."

Mahoney left and slammed the door.

Haven came walking down the street toward Clint. They met up and continued on to the mining office to give Blanchard the news.

"You give Kendall the news?"

"I did," Haven said. "He said he could see to it that the judge wouldn't bother Blanchard anymore."

Clint laughed. "The judge said the same thing to me. Seems they both think they're in charge."

"So what are you gonna do when the federal marshal gets here tomorrow?"

"I'm going to tell him the whole story," Clint said.

"What'd you tell the judge?"

"That I wouldn't say anything to the marshal about him if he cooperated," Clint said, "but I lied."

"What about us shootin' the posse?"

"Well," Clint said, "they weren't deputized, so you shouldn't be in any trouble."

"Yeah, but you shot the sheriff."

"I think with the judge bending the law to suit him," Clint said, "the marshal won't look at the nephew as much of a sheriff."

"I hope you're right."

Clint hoped he was right, too.